Heroes of the Carolyngian Age

Joseph S Samaniego

Copyright © 2020 Joseph Samaniego Smith.

Heroes of the Carolyngian Age

Written by Joseph S. Samaniego.

Published by Joseph S. Samaniego, 2020

Mage's Moon Publishing

This is a work of fiction. Names, characters, businesses, places, events and incidents are either the products of the author's imagination or used in a fictitious manner. Any resemblance to actual persons, living or dead, or actual events is purely coincidental.

No part of this book may be reproduced or transmitted in any form or by any means, electronic or mechanical, including photocopying, recording, or by any information storage and retrieval system, without permission in writing from the publisher.

Maps created by

Joseph S. Samaniego

To my wife and daughters.

To my friends and family.

To the readers.

Table of Contents

The Furies and the Demon Boar...........................1

Godfrey the Conqueror...........................26

The Knight of the Waters...........................41

Rowena and Her Sisters...........................50

There be Dragons!...........................70

About the Author 90

The Furies and the Demon Boar

When the second born child and daughter of Queen Saria, Princess Syrena, was born the trumpets sounded and the Queendom of Amazon rejoiced for days. It was considered a holiday for a princess born in the Queendom. The royal family was as happy as they could ever have been, even Crown Princess Cecilia was happy. At the onset of the pregnancy, the three-year-old princess had made her desire known that she wanted a sister and not a little brother. In her mind, their father, the prince consort, was the only man needed around the royal family. Her mind would stay that way all her life. This story isn't about that, however. One day the two sister's connected fate would come to pass but this story occurred much earlier than that, in the time when both lived comfortable lives within the Queendom of Amazon.

To know the Amazons was to know their different culture from their neighbors in Lotcala or Elysia. Theirs was a matrilineal culture fostered in the ways of the older nomadic lives their ancestors led. Deeply spiritual in their fervent belief in the old gods, the Amazons shunned the encroachments of the missionaries preaching against their own faith. They were warlike in their nature but the days of executing missionaries had long since passed when their allies in Lotcala accepted the Creator. This prompted the Amazons to show tolerance.

In the capital, Verna, Queen Saria ruled with grace, like her mother and grandmothers had done for generations before her. Though much of the fighting during her lifetime was minor and relegated to small border skirmishes, the Amazons kept up their military training through brutal contests of skill and strength. Perhaps one day they would be tested again.

An uneasy peace had settled over the lands of Amazon, Lotcala, Fe and Elysia in the last few years, though some of the distrust of Elysia remained. Truces were in effect, signed a couple generations before the events of this story, and that gave way to some prosperity. Traders opened their wares to long, winding roads that connected the kingdoms and queendom. It was a good time within Central Continent and the queendom rejoiced in the growing wealth. The queen had found some comfort in the peace.

All that changed, however, when the Demon Boar reared its ugly head. Wild boars had always roamed the forests and grasslands of the Central Continent and if they went unchecked, some would grow to large beasts capable of killing humans. That is in fact what this particular boar had become, a man eating boar.

Far in the most remote region of the queendom, north of the Sunset Lake, was a village called Pelagia and that was where the boar had been terrorizing the locals, killing livestock and damaging crops. Should the boar reproduce then the offspring could cause just as many problems and the land would become cursed. Many already stated to call the village cursed. Maidens running off with foreign men from Fe or Elysia brought down disfavor from the old gods or some other demons. The superstitions they held onto, far from the truth of the matter. Still, many looked to the old gods for answers.

It was, however, the first instinct of Queen Saria was to send out some of her best troops from her personal guard. These legionnaires were the finest soldiers that the queendom had to offer. Trained for years in the art of warfare and military strategy, these women were fearsome and ready to lay their lives down for the queendom. Five ventured out to the small village but only one returned.

The boar, it seems, was not a typical feral pig like those found in the Kingdom of Lotcala, long ago brought to the area by the Gota. No, this was the Demon Boar, bred in the fires of the Azufre, the underworld ruled by Malum. Legends had spoken of this beast since the days when the Amazon Queendom was a nomadic people. The oracles told the tales of how the beast was born of dark magic. Therefore, this was a beast that had to be stopped.

The queen was racking her brain on what to do but in the meantime, the oracles in the area began to speak on their outlandish theories about how to stop the beast. More than a few suggested sacrificing the young boys and girls to appease the demon. When the queen heard of this she called for the oracles to be branded as heretics and their tongues removed. The days of human sacrificial offerings was long over but here she feared that the practice could begin again and she was not about to let that happen while she was queen. More soldiers ventured to the village but they too fell to the beast.

Queen Saria was a warrior but not the best in the queendom, she didn't have to be as queen. The title of the best warrior went to the Crown Princess Cecilia, however, she was away on a diplomatic mission to Lotcala. It was her mother's wish that the two nations be bonded through blood and so she was organizing a marriage, her mother's idea since she had been born, between her eldest daughter and King Liam of Lotcala's youngest son, Gabriel. A match that was thought of unfavorably by either participant. Still, it was her duty to venture to Jovag, the Lotcalan capital, to discuss terms. Once there, she found the prince was gone, ventured north to find adventure after being allowed, by his uncle, to graduate a year early from the War Academy. To Cecilia this was a grievous insult that she would carry with her but this wasted trip also left her far away from her lands during their time of need.

Seeing that absence, Princess Syrena, the eighteen-year-old daughter of Queen Saria, stepped in front of her mother's throne and knelt down on one knee. She was wearing her iron cuirass over her linen chiton and iron greaves on her shins. She carried her large round shield, strapped to her back and her ironwood spear in her left hand, her Corinth helm was tucked under her right arm.

"Your majesty, I've come to seek your blessing in ridding the queendom of the Demon Boar before the winter mating season." The princess said, looking to the stone floor. It was the custom when speaking to the queen to avert one's gaze to the floor.

Queen Saria was caught off guard and stood from her marble throne. "You are but eighteen and never tested in a true battle. Why would I send someone so unproven? Stand up and leave this to trained legionnaires." She waved her hand and sat back down.

The throne room murmured and some snickered at the queen's words. Though the queen and her daughters carried weight as royals, Syrena did not hold the same respect amongst her peers as her sister did. This was due to the lack of fighting experience during her time up until this point. However, Syrena was undeterred.

The princess ignored those around her. "Your majesty, I came only as a courtesy, for Pelagia is truly in the province of Caleope. It is therefore my duty as the Vicountess of Caleope to protect my people."

"You are not ready." The queen responded, her voice rising more than normal.

"I was the strongest in the Paideia[1] and I commanded the Herd[2] from there. It is my right to lead this expedition and a matter of my personal honor." Syrena replied, undaunted.

"I've already said what I said. You will remove yourself from my sight!" The queen roared.

"I will not." Syrena never moved and kept her eyes to the floor. "I will not move until you grant me the blessing of Jul and yourself!" Syrena fired back.

Queen Saria rose from her throne. "You are every bit your father." She said, glancing at her husband through the corner of her eye. She could see the man smirking. "You and he might want to be careful with how much you each test me today." Saria walked down from her throne and towards her daughter. She withdrew her sword, a falcata with an ornate hilt of a gorgon's body and head. Saria held the sword gently by the blade in her left hand and presented it to Syrena. The princess raised her head and lowered her spear to the floor. She reached for the hilt and grasped the magnificent sword, the sign of the queen's blessing. "Come back to me." Saria said as Syrena stood.

---

[1] Amazonian military training
[2] The youth brigade of the Amazonian Military

The princess nodded and then took the sword's sheath from her mother's hand and hooked it onto her own baldric. She then retrieved her spear from the ground and left the throne room. Queen Saria stood and watched her youngest daughter fade from her view.

Away from the throne room stood four Amazonian warriors, all in bronze cuirasses and greaves. They wore blue chitons and heavy bronze shields. They were young and still green in the ways of the world. Soon Princess Syrena approached them.

"We ride within the hour!" the princess exclaimed to the delight of the four companions. The five women then rushed off to gather their packs for the journey.

Pelagia was only a one and a half days ride from the capital but the road was teeming with traders and other merchants which made the roads slower than what Syrena and her band would have preferred. Still, the princess was happy to have the company. With here were four of her oldest and most trustworthy friends. In their time in training during their paideia years the five had been known as Furies, mythical beasts thought to have been bred by Guerra, the old goddess of war. The comparison came from their fighting style, grouped and unrelenting.

There were few inns along the roads in the Amazon Queendom and this meant that at night the roadsides would be alight with campfires. Syrena and her band were no different but this was their training, a sitting on the ground around a campfire was a second home. To an Amazonian warrior a camp was a place of bonding and for the Furies this was a chance to unwind to a good meal and laughter.

Althaea, a tall and muscular warrior, took the time to shave her short black hair from her head. An old tradition of warriors going into battle, though the tradition was dying out.

"I don't know why you're doing that." Ino laughed. "That's what our mothers and grandmothers did."

"That's exactly the point!" Althaea responded. Her voice boomed across the campfire to her companions. "We should honor their traditions and then our children will honor ours."

Ino laughed. "If I live long enough to have daughters then I fear for their father, whoever the bastard might end up being." She leaned back against a log and closed her eyes. Another of their companions, Melantho, took her knife and gently pulled at Ino's red hair and quickly sliced an inch off. Ino jumped up while the rest of the group burst out laughing.

"Damn you, Mel!" Ino yelled. She jumped onto her friend and began to punch her. Both rolled until Althaea pulled them apart. Another of the Furies, Mestra, rushed in to steady Melantho from stumbling into the campfire.

Melantho, still laughing, tucked the inch of hair into her pouch. "Something to remember you by when that temper of yours gets the better of you. I'll give it to your daughter's father."

Ino smirked. "Good thing I can back up my temper."

Althaea went back to shaving her head while Mestra went to sit on one of the logs with Syrena. The princess hadn't been paying any attention to the two women fighting, instead thinking of what was to come.

"You should eat princess." Mestra said, pushing a plate of food in front of Syrena.

"You know I hate when you call me that." Syrena replied, taking the offered food.

"It's who you are. I'd be a poor subject of your mother's if I didn't recognize your title." Mestra replied stoically.

"In that case I'd prefer you refer to me as Viscountess."

"Not regal enough." Mestra smiled.

The atmosphere of the camp grew lighthearted as the night wore on and the companions found sleep to be easy that night. The morning sun roused the warriors from their slumber. After a quick meal of bread and cheese, Syrena led the group along the road heading north.

The further north they went the less they saw of merchants and traders.

Ino was the first to speak up. "Should have seen more people. It's been nearly three hours and we haven't seen a soul."

"Not even a farmer taking crops to market." Melantho replied.

"It's a sunny, autumn day. My father would never have left crops sit in the fields or the granary on a day like this." Althaea remarked.

"Maybe they already past." Ino suggested.

Syrena pulled the reins of her horse and brought the animal to a stop. "No." She replied. "The nearest town is along this round south. We passed it just after we left. The next town is Pelagia and it's only a couple miles away. There is something foul keeping the people away." Syrena looked around. She saw smoke from a chimney waft in the distance so she knew people were nearby in the village. "Mestra, what do you feel?"

Mestra rode her horse to the front of the group and closed her eyes. She felt beyond the visible world and felt for anything that wasn't supposed to be there. Mestra was an oracle, like her mother and her grandmother before her, and this meant that she could feel and "see" into the Thin Place beyond the mortal realm.

"There is a darkness over the land ahead. Something there in village is causing the taint to spread over the land." Mestra replied once she broke from her trance but she never turned to her companions.

"Did you see what it was?" Ino asked.

"No but I saw a glimpse of our fates." Mestra replied. She finally turned toward the others. "Some of us will not survive."

Ino and Melantho burst out laughing, drawing a scowl from Mestra. "Okay gloomy!" Ino replied. "We're the fiercest warriors in the queendom and we've killed plenty of boars!"

"That's right!" Laughed Melantho. "This is why you don't have a sword-sister."

Mestra scowl deepened and anger began to take over her. Syrena, seeing the scene stepped in. "She does have a sword-sister." The princess said riding up to Mestra. Ino and Melantho looked at the princess, confused. "Me, you idiots!"

Then it was Althaea's turn to laugh as her two companions shrunk off to the side of the road, embarrassed.

"Mestra, did you feel any living souls?" Syrena asked ignoring the previous scene.

Mestra turned to the princess, still scowling. "Yes, there are people in the village but not many. Something foul has driven many away or worse."

Syrena nodded. "Let's go then but everyone stay vigilant." She led her horse and the group onward, thinking back to what her attendant Mitzudi had told her about the spirits that roamed the lands ages before. The Quarmi woman that had been near Syrena since her birth was well versed in the tales from the ages that had gone by and the changes in the world before their own age. Evil spirits like the Demon Boar were remnants of the magic that had been more powerful in the Arcane Age or Age of the Cold Sun.

The group slowly made their way toward the outskirts of the village, passing rotted crops left to wither in the fields.

"This isn't what I remember from the last time I came." Syrena remarked. They rode on until they made it to the village square and they dismounted at the well in the center of the square.

Althaea looked around but not noticing anyone she called out. "By the queen's orders show yourself to Princess Syrena!" Nothing. Althaea looked to Mestra. "I thought you said there was some life in the village."

"I did. Your loud voice probably scared them." Mestra replied.

Althaea let out a loud 'hmpf'.

Suddenly they heard a soft tone. A harp being played not far away.

Ino began to move to the noise. "It's coming from that house." She pointed.

The group walked over to the wooden house and Syrena slowly pushed the door open. "Hello?" She said aloud. The harp stopped and an elderly woman walked up from a room off to the side.

"Who are you?" The woman asked, raising an eyebrow.

"This is..." Althaea began from behind Syrena but the princess cut her off.

"We're soldiers sent by Queen Saria to stop the boar attacks." Syrena finished.

The old woman chuckled. "Some soldiers tried already. It didn't work out to well for them."

"We're not them." Syrena replied.

"We're better!" Melantho joked.

"Time will tell young one." The woman smirked. "The beast you seek will come in the night. It always does. Come in until then and eat something."

The group accepted the woman's invitation and soon she was preparing a stew in a pot over her hearth. "We used to have more farmers in the village. More farmers meant more foods so forgive me but this is all I can offer." The woman said when she handed the warriors their bowls.

"It is plenty." Mestra said. The others agreed.

Syrena put her spoon down on the table. "Please tell us what you know about this boar."

The woman sat across from the princess and gave a loud sigh. "That damn beast came a few months back and killed a farmer one night as he was calling in his dogs. Worth noting the dogs were killed too. We didn't know it was the boar at first. Not until a few nights later when the village guard saw it. Burning red eyes and almost as big as a horse. Arrows and spears still in its pierced skin." The woman paused to drink some water. "Within a month from there ten more villagers were killed and then warriors came from all around and they too were killed. The queen's legion came and the boar bested them."

"How do you think it came here?" Ino asked.

"I'm no mage or oracle. I can't walk in the mists so I don't have much of a clue." The woman replied.

"It comes at night?" Syrena asked, turning the woman's attention to her.

"Mostly. Once or twice during the day but mostly at night. Any night."

"Then tonight we hunt." Syrena responded.

The warriors all nodded. They knew that later they would be tested. After their meal, they scouted the village, taking advantage of the midday sun. They saw very few people come out of the houses but a couple did tend to small plots and gardens. The day wore on but finally the sunset and darkness fell across the village. Syrena led her fellow warriors out into the night.

Syrena picked up her spear and shield, looking to her companions. "Althaea, you and Mestra will walk with me. Ino, you and Melantho will guard the village."

"Yes my lady." They all replied.

The time had come to do what warriors are meant to do.

Syrena and her group stalked the woods surrounding the village as quietly as they could.

They had hunted all their lives and with their ironwood spears in hand they were confident they would kill the boar. Syrena walked with Althaea and Mestra at each of her flanks, ready to rush in once the boar was cornered.

Ino and Melantho were in the village walking and waiting for any sign.

"So you really don't plan on taking a husband?" Melantho asked.

"What's the point? I'll find a man to bed, have a few daughters and that's that." Ino replied, grinning.

"What if you have a son?"

Ino smirked. "Give him to his father to raise and shown how to be a proper Amazonian man. Do you plan on taking a husband?"

"I do. I remember seeing my parents together and happy and I know the support that a husband can provide is part of that happiness and I'm grateful to have an older brother that I grew up around." Melantho smiled. "I'd like to give my daughters a life like that one day. If I have a son, then I'll raise him to be a proper Amazonian man."

"It's different. Your father, may the gods keep him, was a magistrate and an eupatrid[3], born from a noble family. Fine stock for a man. My mother didn't find much like that and my sisters and I are all from different fathers. That's the life of most of the ergatis[4]. That's why so many of us strive for military glory!"

"That's the old ways." Melantho scolded.

---

[3] The highest class of Amazonian society; Nobility.
[4] The lowest class of Amazonian society; laborers.

Ino stopped walking. "Yes and privilege still rules. Your mother and father were of the same class. They were eupatrids and your mother was a stratego[5]. The rules don't apply to them. They can marry without permission." Ino said. She inched closer to her friend. Ino was taller and leaner than Melantho but Ino was known for having great physical strength and an intimidating nature. Her blue eyes pierced through the eye slits of her Corinth helm. "Like my mother I am in the military not simply because I'm an Amazon but because if I live long enough and rise in the ranks then I can, maybe, count myself amongst the axio[6]."

Melantho pulled her helm off her head, her blond hair falling to her shoulders, and she looked deeply into her friend's eyes. "And, what if I think you're worthy now."

Ino took her helm off. "Then you're a fool." She smiled. "I've done nothing of note."

"You've become my sister you idiot." Melantho laughed along with Ino, punching her arm in jest.

They two shared a hearty laugh when suddenly a strange growling and grunting sound. The two turned and saw the red eyes of their night's hunt.

"Shit!" Ino said putting her helm back on. Melantho did the same and both leveled their spears. Ino gripped her shield in her left hand, Melantho braced herself for an attack.

The boar burst into a run and rushed to the warriors. For such a large beast, its speed was

---

[5] General Rank; part of Nobility.
[6] The officer class of Amazonian military. Considered second class of society.

tremendous and it was heading for Melantho. Ino saw the collision before it could happen and she rammed her left shoulder into her friend, knocking her out of the way and taking the full force of the boar as the beast crashed into her shield.

Ino flew back nearly ten feet. Melantho, who had been dropped to her knees, rose and jabbed her spear point into the boar's hide but it did not penetrate. The boar reared up, front hooves on Ino's sheild and slammed its tusks down on the shield over and over again. Melantho threw her spear to the ground and drew her kopis. She jumped onto the boar and tried to slice at it but the beast kept rearing up and quickly threw Melantho off. The boar looked to where the Amazon warrior had landed and began to walk over to her. Ino, bleeding and with two broken ribs, took that moment to push herself up and slam her shield into the back of boar's head. The heavy blow caused the beast stagger to the left.

Hearing all the commotion, Syrena, Althaea and Mestra emerged from the forest and began to attack the boar with their spears but nothing worked. Melantho was able to get up with Ino's help and in turn she helped her wounded friend away from the fight.

Soon the boar let out a high pitched cry and shoved a large tusk deeply into Althaea's abdomen, right through the bronze armor. In an instant the tusked ripped back out in a bloody spectacle.

Althaea dropped to the ground, clutching her side as the boar ran off, and back into the forest.

* * * * *

"Dammit!" Melantho shouted later on in the old woman's house. "We had the bastard!"

"No we didn't. It had us." Ino winced, trying to lift herself up.

Melantho rushed to her friend's side. "Stay still. You're wounded."

"Yeah, I knew that. How's Althaea?" She gasped, laying back down.

"Syrena and Mestra are wrapping her up now."

Ino looked to her friend. "Wrapping her wound?"

Melantho lowered her head. "No, her body. They are preparing her for the pyre. The wound was too deep and she bled out quickly and died. You had passed out by that time."

Ino began to tear up. "She was a good woman and fine warrior. The queendom is all the lesser for her loss." They were words of honor but part of the warrior's benediction. Her true feelings were kept within.

"I know you two were very close." Melantho said.

"Do you, Mel?"

"Your glances back and forth and I saw the two of you one night entering her tent back in training. You were kissing her. I kind of figured out the rest from there. I said you were my sister. Of course I knew of the two of you. We all did to be honest and we thought you two would be happy." Melantho responded.

"The gods have other plans." Ino remarked. "The boar has to die so that Althaea can be avenged!"

"It will die and Althaea will rest well." Syrena said as she walked into the room.

"What about her rites, Althaea's rites?" Ino asked.

"Mestra is finishing the rites and is sending her soul to Gidoxas. Once the boar is dead we will cremate her and spread her ashes."

Ino nodded. "So, tonight we kill it?"

Melantho shook her head. "No, tonight you rest and we three will kill it."

"No!" Ino screamed. "You will not leave me here!"

"I will not lose another friend!" Melantho yelled. "We will hunt this boar and you will rest. You have to carry on her memory."

Ino scowled at her friend. "Princess are you going to let her…"

Syrena stopped her. "She's only repeating my orders. Someone has to report back, just in case."

"The Queen's Legion? Only one returned." Ino said.

"That is our way. One must live to tell the story." Melantho replied.

"Mestra said some of us would die. Princess you should be the one to…"

"No. I am not injured and I will not bring shame on my family by running when I can still fight."

"And I should? I should be the one to be shamed?"

"What shame, Ino? You saved my life by throwing yourself onto that beast. What shame is there in that?" Melantho asked, sitting down on the bed next to her friend.

Ino quieted and looked to away from Melantho. "The shame of daughter of a lower cast mother. A mother that abandoned the queendom." She said looking back to her friends. "My mother died in some foreign land in the east and we never gave her any damn rites. She left us to make a name for herself and to better her life and ours. She was marked a coward for leaving the army but she knew that she had to, so that we could have something more. The gold she sent home was welcomed but we all eagerly awaited her return more than anything. A return with honor and glory. It never came. Only a few soldiers with a sack of gold and silver, along with her armor. This armor that sits at my bedside! That's my shame. I will not be branded a coward. She never got the chance to prove it but I'll be damned if anyone says the same about me or even thinks it. I will fight this boar and to hell with our ways! If we all die then so be it!" Ino yelled as she rose from the bed.

Syrena looked Melantho and then back to Ino. She could feel pride for her friend and her eyes began to water. Syrena wiped her eyes. "Very well, I'll be honored to die beside you my sister. All of you! The four of us will wait out this beast and attack it tonight." Syrena said.

"She's in no state!" Melantho tried to protest but Syrena put her hand in the air, motioning for her to stop.

Mestra entered the room just then. "The rites have been spoken and the body is ready for the pyre."

"Good." Ino said. "Now let's talk about killing the bastard."

"When was the last time any of you hunted a boar?" Melantho asked.

"Been a while but I remember the trap technique." Syrena replied. "Our spears won't do much good against its hide. We've seen that. This is a different and deadly beast."

"Forgive me princess but fear will make the beast seem bigger than it truly is. My thoughts are different than piercing its sides and back. What about its underbelly?" Melantho said in return. "Just like sinking a blade into the belly to clean it and skin it. We might be able to pierce its stomach."

"Good thought but what about getting under it? I tired that and it didn't work out too well." Ino laughed with a strain on her side.

"We can use ropes." Mestra said. "Make a web of strong ropes and get him tangled up."

"Let's give it a try. We can entrap it and snare him in the ropes against a tree." Syrena said. "But we will need something to draw him in."

"Bait?" Ino asked. "Count me as that. I can't do much else I suppose."

It was a somber gesture but they all agreed. Ino struggled to get out of the bed but she did and with the help of a nearby staff, she made her way out into the square to sit with her fallen friend and lover.

Syrena, Melantho and Mestra went out into the forest, trying to follow the path the boar had taken the night before in getting into the village. Their goal was to set up a rope snare with some thick rope they had found in a barn in the village.

The web they were wrapping around trees and concealed underbrush was given enough slack to be a little bit pliable but still tight enough to restrict the boar's movement. A counterweight was tied several cut ends. These weights would help to ensure that the boar was truly entangled and weighed down. The web was intricate and sturdy, tied around several larger trees for stability. Thinner trees were bent, meant to snap and tighten once the weights were pulled by the boar, while other trees would simply tighten and provide the resistance in the trap.

"If Ino can successfully lure it back this way, then these ropes should be able to trap him." Syrena said, looking at their handy work. "If this works then the boar will not only be trapped but turned towards us so that we will have a clear target in its belly."

"Pray to the grandmothers and the goddess that it'll work then." Mestra replied.

The group went off to sit for a short time with Ino before nightfall. They didn't say a word and the moment was peaceful, but it was fleeting for they knew what they had to do that night.

The moon was full in the sky when the four friends set out into the forests. Ino did her best to keep up but she was hobbled by her injuries. Melantho, however, stayed behind with her until they reached the spot Ino was to stand and wait.

"We'll send him your way. Are you sure about this? That shield you're holding is heavy." Syrena asked.

"Yeah I'm sure. Just bring him to me." Ino responded stoically.

The other three warriors nodded and ran off to their positions. The idea was to drive the boar out of wherever it was hiding and to run it into the trap. They knew that the boar had a taste for flesh so the wounded Ino would be the perfect bait.

To make herself more appealing to the hungry beast, Ino removed her bandages and pulled at the skin around her cut wounds, letting blood flow out. She looked down to her side and she saw the streams of blood begin to run down towards her thighs. "That should do it." She said to herself.

It felt like hours but it was only thirty minutes later that they all heard the shrill cry and grunting of the boar as it emerged from its lair. The bushes rustled as it walked through and they could hear it snorting and rummaging through the ground. It had picked up a scent and now it was searching for the source.

Syrena, Mestra and Melantho watched it move as they sat in their hiding spots. Ino heard the beast moving but she couldn't see it. She picked up her heavy shield and her sword.

"Come on! Come and get me pig!" she yelled, banging on her shield with her sword.

Syrena and the others watched as the boar lifted his head and look into Ino's direction. Suddenly it burst out into a run as it took the bait.

Melantho was the first to pull a rope snare that pulled a large tree low and blocked the boar's path. The beast made a quick turn to the right and Mestra was there pulling her rope and dropping several smaller trees into the boars path. It reared up and turned to the left, avoiding the trees. The two warriors gave chase as the boar rushed past and through a rope web. Mestra, pulled a cord that was lying near the web and the ropes tightened behind the boar.

"Once Syrena pulls her ropes then he'll be trapped." Melantho said.

Just then the boar burst through the brush and it was straight in line with Ino. It look her in the eyes and she sneered at the boar.

"Come on bastard and get your dinner!" She roared.

The boar broke out into a sprint as it rushed through and Syrena watched its pace. She waited and kept a firm grip on the ropes in her hands. She waited for the exact moment that the boar was in place and just as it put its hooves down she jerked the ropes with all of her strength. Ino had raised her shield to cover herself and the boar was just a few feet away but it was there, dangling in the air as Syrena gripped the ropes and held them with all her might.

"The weights! They didn't work!" Syrena desperately held on but she felt the boar's weight begin to give the ropes slack. Mestra and Melantho came up and helped pull, tighten the ropes that had snagged the boar. Ino stood and walked over to her friends, tied one of the ropes to her shield before sliding it through the middle of two pines. She fixed it snuggly behind the tree to allow it to hold the weight.

"That should hold him." Ino remarked. They all went back to the beast as it was suspended from the ground and looked at the prey.

"Looks like any other boar, just huge." Mestra said. She was right, however. The boar was larger than any other they had ever seen. At least half a ton in weight.

"These ropes won't hold for much longer the way it's moving." Syrena remarked.

The princess took her spear from her back and lined up with the boar's heart and thrusted the point as deeply as she could. The boar squealed and blood spurted out frantically. Syrena pulled the spear from the boar and more blood erupted from the beast. It still squealed and tried to move but the fight drained from its body much like its life did. Soon the boar ceased to move anymore and the warriors counted the blessings that it was over.

"My spear, I'll drag it out." Syrena said.

"We'll help." Mestra added.

"A kill made by a Fury is a glory for all Furies. Living and dead." Meantho continued.

"For Althaea." Ino said to finish.

The four warriors drug the boar's body to the village square where a few of the remaining villagers came to greet them with cheers and wine. The warriors, along with the villagers all cast blessings to the old gods and took the boar and cleaned it so they could cut the meat off. The villagers took a large share of the meat while Syrena took the skin, Mestra and Melantho each took a tusk with them. Ino took the skull of the boar, boiling it so it would be clean and she wrapped it up for the return trip. The night after the boar's death, the warriors said their final goodbyes to Althaea and burned her upon the funeral pyre, villagers in attendance. They then took her ashes and scattered them to the winds as their mothers and their grandmothers would have done.

It was a silent journey home. Although, the sisters had a few days of rest after the boar was killed, Ino winced with each footstep of her horse as they traveled home. The four warriors entered the capitol city of Verna to a somber atmosphere. The crown princess had returned but the marriage had not been agreed on. Syrena soon learned why and couldn't help but to smile. She and Prince Gabriel had always shared a bond and it was her secret heartbreak that tore at her during the marriage talks. Now it seemed that at least some good news came from the spectacle.

Walking into the throne room, the four warriors were greeted by the queen's guards but were allowed to pass. Syrena and her fellow warriors walked up to the throne and knelt before it, dropping their weapons to their sides.

"My daughter is now a grown woman and warrior." The queen said as she sat upon her throne. "A boar's skin on her back."

"Tusks and skull to my fellow warriors." Syrena replied.

"Princess Syrena the Boar." Cecilia remarked which drew laughter from around the throne room. Syrena wasn't sure if it was respect or a jest at her expense.

"She killed the Demon Boar. Something, even the Queen's Legion could not do." Ino said in response. "A Fury died in the hunt and she avenged her, sending her soul to Gidoxas with honor and glory." The room quieted down.

"Then we must honor a fallen sister." Cecilia said with a scowl. "Glory to the Furies!" The crown princess said. The throne erupted in a cheer as the four stood and walked out.

Later the four warriors sat in a tavern and drank to the memory of their friend.

"What now?" Melantho asked. "Join a legion?"

"That's the order I received." Syrena replied. "You are all welcomed to join me. Because of your accomplishment you all have been given the choice."

Ino smiled. "I'll be at your side princess." She said, raising her tankard.

"As will I." Melantho put in.

"Forgive me princess." Mestra began. "But I must journey south. When I scoured the Thin Place for the boar previously I felt something odd. Something unseen even by me." She looked off for a moment before returning to the princess' gaze. "I need to venture to Kalisadad to learn from their guild. They might have the answers that I can't find here."

"And what about your oath to the guild here." Ino asked.

Mestra looked to her friend. "I've arranged that already. My younger sister, Morea, will fulfill my oath until she can take her own oath. I plan to return before that happens, though."

Syrena nodded. "Then let Jul protect and keep you sister."

The group continued to drink and celebrate until the sun began to rise in the east and they had all passed out in the tavern. Their last toast was to their reunion and future glories for the Furies.

Godfrey the Conqueror

Uffe was king of Gotistan in name only. Most of his days were simply spent in the woods; hunting and being one with the natural world, just like he would do prior to his days on the Central Continent helping his cousins reconquer Tresha. In the old country, he was placed on the throne to rule but he shunned the right. Still, it was his in name and title based on his blood, no matter for the fact that his local jarls and lords really ruled behind his back.

Uffe's eldest son, Godfrey Uffesson, was sent to Tresha to lead a force of warriors out into the grasslands to subdue the tribes that had not joined the Gota previously. This included the still aggressive Quarmi. Though some of the magical race had joined up with Theodorif and then formed a separate domain, many from Nara wanted vengeance and they saw the warriors from Tresha as the focus of that vengeance. The Treshans knew they would need help to fight off the horde that was coming.

After being invited to join a crusade against the Quarmi from Nara and the unruly Grasslanders, Godfrey sailed with nearly two thousand Gota warriors to River Port. The growing port city was a wealthy jewel along the coast of the Central Continent. From there he set out to the newly crowned King of Tresha, Rolf Fenirsson.

King Rolf was not the greatest of kings but Tresha was being rule unofficially by the jarls of the kingdom. This gave the nobility the bulk of the authority and once arrived, Godfrey took his place among them. Such a life suited him perfectly fine and so his days were spent in battle. That was the beginning. Once stepping off the ship and leaving River Port, the Gota warrior saw little reason to farm or tend to livestock. He was there to bring the lands to its knees and bow to the might of the Gota. King Rolf saw a use for his cousin within days and so Godfrey was sent to the northern borders of Tresha, just south of Orleuns and there he first encountered the Quarmi.

The first battle told the proud Gota warrior all he needed to know of the magical race; they were worthy foes and honorable in defeat. However, they were followers of the Creator and not the old gods. This meant that Godfrey would be their enemy for as long as he had a breath. Now anyone would be forgiven in thinking that the greatest accomplishment of Godfrey's was being crowned king of both Tresha and Gotistan when he was in his middle age, but for Godfrey his crowning glory came in battle. The Battle of the Orleuns Plains.

By the time Godfrey had reached his thirtieth year he was already a jarl in the northern reaches of Tresha. His father was dying and his cousin was more concerned with banquets than conquest. However, for Godfrey the goal had always been to carve out more land to call his own. In the lands north of Tresha he could make a jarldom all his own and be far enough away from his cousin to rule as if he was the king himself. The only problem was the hostile and numerous Quarmi that called that area home. They would have to fall in line under his rule or be removed. He simply didn't care which.

Upon a high hill Godfrey looked out over the field that he knew would soon be covered with the blood of brave warriors. He smiled at the thought of the honor that each fallen warrior would share in and the glories that the victors would rejoice.

"Jarl Godfrey, our scouts have spotted the Quarmi's advance troops on the eastern borders." The attendant Finn reported. "Our own forces are ready to meet them head on."

Godfrey turned away from the fields and smiled at his friend. "If we defeat them here then we will have complete control of these lands?"

Finn nodded. "Yes sir."

"Not just that but my own lands would then be equal to the king's." Godfrey continued.

"Aye jarl. No other lord or jarl would compare in lands. They already can't compare in strength." Finn said.

"Then let's win this day and show those other lords what it truly means to be Gota!" Godfrey grinned menacingly.

Godfrey traveled down to his army's encampment, nearly fifteen thousand men and a few women standing by, ready for the word to mobilize. Godfrey was almost giddy at the thought of finally facing the last of the four great Quarmi generals, Ultida Kagesuke.

Kagesuke was a veteran of the previous war against the Yendis during the Gota invasions. However, once the schism between the Quarmi loyal to the queen and the those wishing to continue to stay allied to the Gota occurred, Kagesuke chose to remain with his queen, though in truth, he did not follow the same traditions. Godfrey had faced the other three generals' armies but never encountered the warrior generals in battle. Prior to meeting with Godfrey each had taken their lives as a form of retaining honor.

Godfrey despised the notion and he sought to reach Kagesuke before he could do the same.

For the cultural differences that existed between the people, Godfrey could not understand the ideas of committing such an act for the sake of honor. To die in battle was what Godfrey, and many other Gota, thought of as the highest form of personal honor. "Dying upon the field of battle with a sword in one's hand meant that each man or woman died on their feet."

Godfrey mounted his horse and rallied his forces together as they rode and marched out of the encampment to meet with the Quarmi army.

"This will be the end of it all Finn." Godfrey remarked as they rode side by side. "Make sure we reach Kagesuke. I want him alive."

"Aye jarl." Finn thought for a moment. "Sir, the previous generals...why?"

Godfrey shook his head. "I can't say for certain but I've heard enough tales to think it is part of the Quarmi idea of an honorable death."

Godfrey was a student of war and it was his goal, after conquering all the lands he could reach, to learn as much from his advisories as possible. He did not wish to kill them simply because they fought against him. He would gladly let every enemy live to old age but with the Quarmi he was seeing that their leaders would choose to die rather than to face the defeat.

The Quarmi advance was larger than the Gota had seen thus far and Godfrey knew it was the remnants of their once great cavalry. At the head of the army was Kagesuke, leading as a warrior would. Godfrey smiled. Coming down from the hill his army had camped on, Godfrey broke out in a charge, his horsemen following behind.

Godfrey's cavalry was heavier, not only the men and their armor but also the horses were larger. This gave the Gota an advantage during a full charge but it made them slower when compared to the much more agile Quarmi horses, which were a smaller breed.

The crash of horses, armor and iron echoed through the valley. The Quarmi had mounted a charge of their own but against the armored horsemen of the Gota they were pushed back. Godfrey rode through the line with little resistance until he met with the Quarmi phalanx.

With their frontline in shambles, the phalanx was their pride. The Quarmi cavalry was all but decimated but their spearmen forming into a phalanx was still as strong as ever. Godfrey rode back and rallied his horsemen behind the enemy riders. He ordered an attack at their riders, ignoring the phalanx until his own spearmen and infantry could reach him. The experienced Gota leader, along with his fellow riders, cut through the Quarmi riders with little trouble. He noticed that the task was much too easy compared to what he fought previously.

"They sent many of their riders to the phalanx!" he yelled. "Return to the shield wall!"

A wall of Gota shields had formed up and stood in that nearly unbreakable formation on the battlefield. Godfrey led his riders back to the line and formed in with them. He saw the Quarmi riders do the same. His suspicions were proving true as more Quarmi dismounted and lined up amongst the phalanx.

"They want this to be a ground battle. So be it." Godfrey said, lining up with his men. Across the plain he could see Kagesuke lining up with his men. "He takes the lead. That's a warrior!" Godfrey exclaimed. The Gota leader urged his men forward at a slow pace so they could stay in line and fight as a single unit.

Kagesuke held his phalanx in place while watching the Gota men inch closer. "Hold!" He yelled.

Before long, both armies were within a spear's length and vying for position. The ground was getting trampled as each side pushed, dirt was muddying with falling blood. While the Gota could win the day on horse, on foot with two spear lines, the Quarmi had regained a balance with the numbers.

Godfrey spurred his men on further and harder. "Push men!" He knew that the Quarmi had a strong line but he was caught off guard by the strength he was facing. "Harder!"

The Quarmi took a moment to strike with their second line pikemen. The attack struck true and many of the Gota fell to the deadly assault. Another attack came in the same fashion of pikes and spear points ripping at the Gota warriors' flesh. Godfrey snarled at the successful attacks and ordered a push. With a massive heave the Gota shield wall slammed into the Quarmi Phalanx and knocked the poised soldiers back several paces.

It was enough to give the Gota a fighting chance again as they rushed forward in a quick advance. Gota warriors brandishing axes and swords took the short opportunity to hack and slash at the Quarmi soldiers. Many of the Quarmi fell but others took their place. It would go on like this for much of the day and Godfrey knew as much. Both commanders, for that matter, knew the winner of this battle would be the general that withstood the entire battle. This would be a battle where every inch mattered and no second could be wasted.

The two lines of warriors clashed into one another again as spears and pikes thrust forward from both sides in a desperate attempt to weaken the other. Dusk crept over the plain and both sides were weary from the intense fighting. Nothing had stopped the battle but soon the commanders were calling for their own lines to retreat. The battle would have to wait for one more day at least.

"That damn Kagesuke is a strong warrior. This has not been the battle that I had expected to fight." Godfrey smiled as he entered his tent. "Post double guards." He ordered. One of his guards rushed out to relay the order.

"He is much more of a leader than we've witnessed." Finn remarked while pouring water for Godfrey and himself. A woman brought in some wine and began to pour it. "Kagesuke is a different breed of Quarmi."

"I must speak with him!" Godfrey exclaimed from his chair. He took an offered cup of wine from the woman before pulling her down onto his lap. The woman gasped but she did not protest. Serving the jarl was a nightly occurrence either with her or any other woman.

Finn smiled. "Then we should invite him to our camp. We might not get the chance to meet with him after the battle."

Godfrey considered his second in command's words. The truth behind them was evident. "Then let's send out an invitation immediately."

Finn nodded and left the tent. As he walked out he could hear the woman begin to giggle.

* * * * *

Arranging a meeting between the two leaders was difficult but after sometime a table and chairs were set out with candles and torches in the middle of the battlefield. Guards from both sides took their posts as the respected leaders walked up and sat at the table.

"You've invited me to dine with you in the midst of our fallen brothers. Why?" Kagesuke asked as he sat down across from Godfrey.

Godfrey smiled. "I couldn't think of a better place for two warriors and it is neutral territory. Would you have rather come to my tent?"

Kagesuke shook his head. "This will do. What did you wish to discuss?"

"To the point. I like that." Godfrey commended. "General, you and I are warriors and I have always wanted to speak with my opponents. I learn from them and until I came here there was never an enemy I did not speak to prior to his or her defeat. Perhaps even prior to mine. However, your fellow Quarmi have not wished to wait to speak to me and instead kill themselves prior the end of the battle." Godfrey pour some wine into his cup. "Why is that?"

"A defeat such as what you gave to them offers little redemption other than to die in battle. This was their choice to keep their honor. To be a good leader, one must die on the inside so that they can be prepared to die in battle. Before I walk onto the battlefield, my soul is ready."

Godfrey scowled at the answer. "That's not honor. Yes, dying in battle is honorable but taking your own life because of the defeat is cowardly. I am not dumb enough to think that I'll die peacefully in a bed in some lofty castle. I'll die in battle by someone who bests me and that is how I see fit to die. I've led armies that have lost battles, not many, but I have lost battles and then I went on to win the war. My honor can be my legacy for whatever children I might bear."

"It is our way. I've known defeat but some defeats are not like others. Some are worse." Kagesuke replied while taking a cup and pouring his own wine. "My father fell in battle to the Orleuns army and he died as you said a warrior most die but I feel little honor in that personally. My grandfather wore his own defeat as a mark of shame until he took his own life after a costly battle and for that I feel no honor. The old gods, I feel, do not reward us for the outcomes of battles for this is not our true honor. They only reward in the honor we make ourselves."

Godfrey's eyes perked up. "You follow the old gods?"

Kagesuke nodded. "Yes. Is that a surprise?"

"I thought the Quarmi were followers of the Creator."

"The Creator is in the lives of many of my brothers and my queen will gladly kill any who don't follow him but a few of us are allowed our separate beliefs because of what we contribute."

Godfrey nodded. "What do you contribute?"

"I lead her army or at least what is left of it. If I fall in this battle and return to Nara then I will face a very public execution for my faith." Kagesuke said. "Many of my men will not mourn for me because of it but they follow me now knowing that I am the reason we have the lands that we still have to defend."

"I see." Godfrey paused to drink his wine. "You can always join another army or become a mercenary."

Kagesuke shook his head. "That is not my way. I will take my execution with honor for the old gods. There is a freedom in following their way and in knowing the outcome."

Godfrey nodded. "Then tell me about you. What do you think it is to be a warrior?"

"For me that is simple. To live and breathe the air as if the next sword swing is your last. To honor your opponent as you honor your comrades and to fight as equals."

"That simple?"

"For me it is. What about you General Godfrey?"

"Now that's a bit more complicated. I respect and admire your thoughts but for me it is something a bit more tangible. I do indeed feel that there is honor to being a warrior but also there is something that has to be gained. Three things. Knowledge is the first. Win or lose, we will gain knowledge from the experience. Honor is the second and that is something you firmly understand but the third." Godfrey chuckled. "That's the tricky one because that's the one that you only get when you are the victor. The spoils."

Kagesuke skewed his eyes at the Gota warrior. "You consider being a warrior having to do with what you win?"

"I do, it is part of the glory. Again, we don't always win but when we do, those spoils give us incentive." Godfrey replied.

Kagesuke took a sip of water. "Have you fought in many battles?"

Godfrey smiled. "I have." His smile fell into a frown. "Too many."

"Here in this land?"

Godfrey drank some wine and shook his head. "No." He said after putting his cup down. "In my younger days I fought in the southern islands of Zaragoza against the Sea People and in the north against the painted faces."

"The painted faces?" Kagesuke asked in wonder, leaning closer. "I've heard they are fearsome people."

"They are." Godfrey replied. "They fight with older weapons but they are deadly. Some are friendly but there are worse things in the north. The warriors we call the painted faces call themselves the Nimatew People."

Kagesuke leaned back. "Nimatew? Fascinating, and you made friends with these people? I hear they take trophies of skulls."

"Some do and I did make some friends. Enough to recruit a few in my men here." Godfrey looked over and pointed to a darker skinned warrior behind him. The man had a black paint covering the top half of his face and red paint on the lower half. Other markings covered the skin that was visible, a large knife hung at his waist. "That's Stakwiah. His name means Great Hawk, he is a Warchief to the Black Moon, and many of them are here with me."

"They followed you?"

"They are a small tribe of people, known in their homeland as Croatoan, and they were being run off by another tribe. After we helped them, some decided to join me on my quest. Stakwiah has taken many skulls as trophies. Many of those skulls are from the Inini Midjin, the painted faces call them men eaters. They ride large horses and attack villages and kill anything in sight, eating flesh raw. They dishonor the spirits of the world. So keeping the skulls is a way to avenge their fallen people. Their faith allows such things."

"Their faith. An old god?"

Godfrey shook his head. "No, they have a different faith based on spirits and the natural world. They feel the souls of every being all around them."

Kagesuke smiled. "Amazing." He leaned back. "You learned their language then?"

"I did."

"Amazing!" Kagesuke replied with a bit more excitement than he had shown earlier. "Could you teach another?"

"We only have the night."

Kagesuke's mood changed. "That is true and the night is growing short." The Quarmi leader turned his head and then looked back to Godfrey. "Should I lose tomorrow, you wish me to face you after the battle?"

"Of course."

"Part of why Quarmi commit a saving grace is because of a lack of purpose, or maybe a perceived one."

Godfrey nodded knowingly. "You want me to offer something? A purpose?"

"Something like that. I'd prefer not to end this life so soon. I've done nothing but battle for my queen but she is not the woman that she claims to be." Kagesuke remarked solemnly.

"Let's see what tomorrow brings." Godfrey smiled. Kagesuke returned the smile and the two soon returned to their camps.

* * * * *

The next day was hell for both armies. The two walls of warriors clashed with a force that sent men and Quarmi to the ground, only to be stomped on by anyone close, friend of foe. Around midday the lines broke apart and a full melee erupted between the combatants, leaving any organization behind.

The fight was so severe that many warriors were becoming blind with sweat and blood running into their eyes. Godfrey attacked with reckless abandon as did the Quarmi warriors. Few found any mercy on the terrible field that day and many of the Gota saw the true strength of the Quarmi as they fell to the swift blades. Godfrey pushed his men on with his example, hacking and slashing at any Quarmi that came close. His shield, bloody from bashing it into his foes, was cracked and breaking but the Gota leader paid little attention to it. He simply threw it aside when in split in two pieces.

Kagesuke had taken up a naginata, a pole arm with a long blade, and was defending his wounded comrades. He stood near a pile of Gota warriors, fallen to his deadly weapon. Several other Quarmi had defended their position with yumi longbows and were holding their ground but the Gota were closing in quickly. Godfrey found the Quarmi general with ten of his men, surrounded by the corpses of over a hundred Gota warriors. The Gota leader stopped and called for his men to cease.

As he approached Kageuke's last stand, Godfrey ordered his men to stop fighting and Kagesuke halted his own soldiers. "You've held out as much as you can general." Godfrey remarked as he lowered his sword.

"We can do more." Kagesuke replied and his men cheered around him.

"To what end? What purpose does that serve?"

Kagesuke, still holding his naginata in front of him. "My men will die for me and I will gladly die for them."

"But will you live for them?" Godfrey countered. He sheathed his sword. "Go north and find the Roanoac people. They are Stakwiah's wife's people and they will give you a warrior's purpose. The Roanoac are a brave people but they are not as strong as the men eaters." Kagesuke eyed Godfrey carefully as the Gota warrior spoke.

"Why would you not go back yourself?" Kagesuke asked, lowering his polearm.

"A shaman of the Black Moon told me that it wasn't my destiny to stay there or to even return. My path is here, but he said a grey warrior will walk the rest of the path I had begun. I believe that to be you."

Kagesuke looked confused at the words, spoken as if it was prophetic.

Godfrey smiled. "You are the only Quarmi that spoke with me and wanted something more than to die in battle. Honorable as it is, you recognized that there is something more for you out there. This may be it, your destiny."

Kagesuke smiled. "Destiny." The two warriors exchanged smiles and shook hands, ending the conflict.

* * * * *

Time went by and the legend of Godfrey became well known after that last victory over the Quarmi. One day he would become King of Tresha and Gotistan and his rule would be marked by an uneasy peace amongst the jarls. Many did not appreciate a man from Gotistan leading them but they would never dare challenge Godfrey.

However, the legend of Kagesuke was not as familiar to many on the Central Continent. That did not mean that the Grey Warrior was not known. In the north the mysterious Grey Warrior and his ten companions were champions and when an aged siren stepped onto the shore of the Northern Continent, it was Kagesuke who was there to greet her.

The Knight of the Waters

Sir Rickard Greenfield took off his helm as he huffed and puffed. His chest and abdomen heaved under his iron scale and leather armor, but he did what he could to steady his breathing. He looked across the field and saw the river that separated what was left of his army and the vast army of the Elysian king, Gerald. He thought back to the previous couple of days and to the events that led up to this moment.

As the son of the Baron of Greenfield, Rickard had been training for combat since his youth. That was the traditional role of the noble born sons, even for the commoners, the males of society were meant to fight for their overlords. This meant that Rickard was no different and now at twenty three years old he was sent out leading his father's men, since his father was too invalid in his senior years to lead. One day soon Rickard's older brother would be the baron and the true leader of the army, but until then it was up to Rickard. As a knight, he was a warrior with tremendous skill in swinging a sword, so much so that many dared to say he was the greatest swordsman in the entire kingdom. He had yet to be bested in a duel but he was still young and Elysia had its own famed warriors.

It was a sunny day when the young knight rode off with a sizeable force under his father's banner. Fate would have him meet the Elysians at the river near an area he had hunted in during his youth. It was an area he felt at home in but he prayed to the Creator that the land would stay peaceful in the coming days. If he had his way, he and his men would stay out of the bulk of the fighting.

"The supply wagons will have to come this way. This river is the most abundant source of freshwater for nearly thirty miles and this crossing is the shallowest spot for nearly twice that distance." Rickard said as he dismounted from his horse. He looked to the other officers nearby. "Have the men begin setting up a simple palisade and start digging in here. Once they reach the other bank we will begin our attack."

The manor lords of Estan and Curr had followed Rickard to the river, breaking from the main force. All in an effort to cut off the supply train of the King Gerald but they hadn't expected to meet with the famed ruler himself.

King Gerald was an older ruler but one that was battle tested against almost every baron that King Torvin of Lotcala had under him. Even though many of the Lotcalans looked at the Elysians as a less than hardy folk and weaker in martial skill, Gerald carried a higher level of respect. He was a warrior that had yet to be bested in battle and he had fought off many of the Lotcalan advances, even winning land against the mighty kingdom. That was the land that Sir Rickard Greenfield intended to reclaim.

A couple days passed before the sentries reported seeing dust being kicked up in the distance and the sound of marching feet.

"They're close." Rickard said once he received the report but as he ventured close to the palisade he found the situation was much different than he had thought. Though still a ways off in the distance, Rickard could tell by the sound of the march and the amount of dust in the air that it wasn't a simply supply train of wagons but an entire army.

Rickard looked out over the river as the plume of dust grew higher. "Damn." He whispered to himself. Turning back to the manor lords. "Send out messengers to the baron's heir and tell him that King Gerald's main force is coming this way."

The manor lords did as they were ordered and soon four messengers rode off but the Elysian king was close and rest of the Greenfield army was at least a week away.

That night, the opposite bank from Sir Rickard's camp lit up with hundreds of campfires and silhouettes moved through the darkness. Thousands of men rested near the cool flowing waters of Moonstone River. It was a river of crisp water that was known to be a source of moonstones, an important gem to the mages of the world. Rickard saw the stones glow in the full moon as he looked across to the enemy camp. He knew that soon the river would run red with the blood of many dying warriors.

His prophetic thoughts began to materialize as the first wave of fighting began at first light when Greenfield archers rained down a barrage of arrows on the Elysian engineers as they set to work constructing a wooden bridge so that they could cross the river. The river may have been shallow but the need to haul heavy carts meant that the bridge was in dire need. Soldiers with tower shields ran up to provide cover for the engineers and other workers. Rickard watched but he knew that his men had a limited number of arrows and the numbers game would catch up to him sooner or later.

"Begin working on more fortifications here and shore up our own palisade." Rickard ordered his workers. "They will finish that bridge and come across but use our arrows to slow their work until our own defenses are complete."

Rickard was right about slowing the Elysians down and his men had finished before the Elysians attacked, but just barely. Greenfield spearmen clashed over the makeshift bridge, a low bridge just above the water line, as the Elysians came over the water. With a strong phalanx, the soldiers from Greenfield held their position even after multiple charges from their foes. The day wore on and night soon fell but neither side wanted to give an inch. Both pushed and tried to move the others; either back across the bridge or off of it and into the water.

King Gerald had hundreds more men than Sir Rickard and it showed as the night wore on and fresh Elysian soldiers were called up to relieve the weary front lines. The Lotcalans did not have such an advantage. Their tired and weary soldiers had to stay at their posts for as long as they could raise their spears. Still, the silver lining coming through was the news that soldiers from King Torvin were on their way, however, they were nearly five days away. This meant that Rickard had to contend with an onslaught of the best warriors that the Kingdom of Elysia had to offer. Sir Rickard also had very little faith in the warriors from King Torvin, because although he had sent word for the Third Legion he was being sent King's Guards! The lackeys that the barons had refused to let join their barony armies.

Sir Rickard watched from the ramparts of his earthen fort and wondered where the love of the Creator had gone as he looked out on the carnage of his men, brothers in arms, being slaughtered.

"We have to stop this." One of the soldiers from behind Sir Rickard said but the young knight did not pay any attention to him.

Their sacrifice was a necessary evil. Their stand meant that King Gerald was slowed in his advance and the Lotcalans would have time to mount a more sizable defense. Rickard cursed his luck that it came at the expense of his warriors, his friends, his brothers in arms.

"Enough of this!" Rickard shouted. "Sound the retreat." He finished before walking towards his horse.

The Greenfield soldiers fell back in as orderly a retreat as they could but the Elysians took the time to push further. They continued their progress until they saw the white flag in Rickard's hand, a call went out to the Elysians for their forces to cease their advance.

Sir Rickard, in his full iron and leather lamellar armor, trotted his horse onto the bridge and he stood in the center, like a statue poised in the middle of a market square. Soon King Gerald rode up to the young knight.

"Sir. I hope you are seeking to surrender and allowing my army and I passage over this river." Gerald smiled.

"No, your grace. I'm here to issue to you or a champion of your choosing a challenge." Rickard replied with a grimace.

Gerald was understandably taken back. "On what terms?" The king asked.

"You, or your champion, will duel against me and if I win you pull your army back to Elysia and if you win I'll pull my army out." Rickard replied.

Gerald laughed at the stimulation. "And why should I accept? My army is superior and is at the advantage. I only called for the cease to grant you this audience as a courtesy among warlords."

"I thought that you'd say something like that but what will you tell your men when you return to them and they ask what our discussion was about? Will you tell them you refused a challenge? A challenge from another noble?" Rickard chided. "Might be that they would look at you as fearful for your life against a younger man. Forgive me your grace but I only speak thusly as a noble would to another of noble blood."

"You might be a noble but you're a whelp of a man with no thoughts to his betters."

Rickard rolled his eyes at the insult. "A whelp I may be but you are sounding more and more like a coward, afraid of dueling someone younger. Are you feeling a bit more fatigued these days your grace?"

Gerald sneered. "Do you honestly think that you are worthy to stand against me? You're Sir Rickard Greenfield, correct?" Rickard nodded. "Your brother was bested by me and now your father sits feeble awaiting the day I put the rest of your family out of its misery! You have one more brother but before I reach him I will take your head. That way when I reach your father I can show him what he wrought!"

"Then you accept?" Rickard replied without emotion.

Gerald growled in anger before turning his horse and riding back to his line. "This boy as challenged me to a duel! Should he win then we will pull our army out and back to Elysia!" A collective grumble went over the king's warriors.

"Hear me now and hear my acceptance of this term. However, once I win, we will continue unimpeded upon Greenfield and then Jovag."

Rickard dismounted his horse and gave it a smack on its rump to send it back to the Lotcalan ramparts. He turned to face Gerald and drew his sword. Sir Rickard carried a spatha, roughly a meter in length and a round wooden shield with his family arms painted on it. He walked forward and peered through the eye holes of his helm, an iron guard covered the upper half of his face but left his jaw exposed, he could see the king walking towards him ready to duel.

Raising his shield, Rickard crept forward as Gerald lunged in with a high strike from his war mace that connected with devastating force on Rickard's shield. The younger man staggered backward but he maintained his footing on the bridge. It was clear that Gerald, a large man by most standards, was the stronger of the two, Rickard knew he would have to defeat him with agility.

Gerald went to strike again but Rickard moved out of the way and swung his sword at the king's legs, slicing a deep wound into the man. The king let out a yell but still kept up his own attack on the Lotcalan knight. Rickard jumped back but lost his footing and fell back onto the bridge, rolling away just as the heavy mace came down next to his head.

"I told you boy, you are no match for me!" Gerald taunted.

Rickard made his way to his feet and threw his shield at Gerald. The king had to throw his own shield up to block it and just as he did Rickard cut at the king's chainmail with a hard strike. The sword glinted off the mail but the force of the swing made Gerald step back. Rickard kicked the larger man in the stomach and sent him crashing in the shallow water below.

Rickard stood atop the bridge for a moment and watched his opponent struggle to stand up. He prayed to himself that he would concede defeat but once on his feet, Gerald looked up to Rickard and taunted him even more.

"Are you afraid to fight me here in the water?!" Gerald spat out blood. "Are all Greenfield men so dainty?"

Rickard jumped down from the low bridge and brought his sword up defensively just as Gerald went to strike but Rickard parried the swing and threw his shoulder into the man. Giving himself some space, Rickard slammed the pommel of his sword down of Gerald's helmed head and then bashed into him with his shoulder again.

Staggered, Gerald tried to move forward toward the young knight but Rickard swung high and slashed at the king's exposed neck, sending his head down to the shallow river.

Cheers went up from the Lotcalan side and silence echoed across the bank where the Elysians stood in shock. Soon that shock began to turn into anger but their commanders were men of honor.

Though angry and saddened the Elysian commanders took control of the situation quickly to uphold their king's words. "Our king lost a fair contest to a better swordsman." One commander said, coming out into the water to stand over the king and to calm his men. "Who here is man enough to help me carry our fallen king back to the capital for a hero's burial?!" The commander yelled. Many walked up and Lotcalans came over to guard their own leader.

A circle of Greenfield spearmen rushed to Rickard and allowed him to back out of the water and back to his on ramparts. He was tired and winded but relieved. He had won the day and bought time for his army and the kingdom's, though he knew that the war was far from over and his skill would be called upon again soon.

Slowly the Elysians did as they agreed and within a couple days their army had returned south to their capital of Gib. While the rest of the Lotcalan kingdom learned of the deed of Sir Rickard, many of his men and those that would soon hear the tale, began to echo shouts of the brave Knight of the Waters, the heroic Sir Rickard who defeat the King of Elysia and saved the Kingdom of Lotcala!

Rowena and Her Sisters

Frost crept over the ground in the growing darkness of the mercenary camp. There were a few campfires burning but the orders from the captain were clear; keep the fires to a minimum. This would help the eyes to adjust to the darkness. A part from the fires, the camp was built up with meticulous care and for efficiency. Rowena, the captain of the mercenary band, saw to that. The half dwarf and human daughter of King Charles of Lotcala did not accept anything less than the best from her band of warriors. She had been raised by a warrior king and queen, her stepmother Sirie made sure to train her well during her time in the Lotcalan War Academy. It was that rigid structure that made her into the woman and the leader that she was.

Rowena's first year in the academy saw her take the most discipline and even a few more floggings compared to her fellow classmates. Missteps would result in true military discipline since these youths were being trained to hardened soldiers. However, some wondered if the queen in her role as the headmistress of the academy was enjoying the discipline that her stepdaughter received.

Queen Sirie had picked Rowena to lead the class and for every failure of the class, she'd pay the price. Soon, however, Rowena began to demand perfection from her classmates and when she took a beating, they in turn would take one. Eventually the class, which was the first class, had become a well-oiled machine and Sirie couldn't have been prouder of her stepdaughter. Not that she'd ever tell her that. It had been Sirie's goal to turn Rowena into a formidable warrior and leader, who would one day command the forces loyal to her younger half-brother.

Rowena, however, had other plans before being called by her father into a political marriage with a foreign noble. Part of her believed that all the political marriage talk was just her father trying to ease her stepmother's concerns. While King Charles legalized land and title inheritance for women, he never fully legitimized Rowena. This didn't stop him from acknowledging her and showing his love for her but he felt not legitimizing her was safer. Rowena stewed over it but there was little she could do. She loved her brothers and her homeland, she would never betray either. However, she was a threat and she knew the rumors of how her stepmother dealt with threats. Leaving was her best option.

Besides, she had a hard enough time in the years prior to forming her band. *The Dwarven Princess of Lotcala*, as she was called due to her looks and blood by those wishing to scorn her, decided to change her future by forming a mercenary band of warrior women. They all had graduated from the academy with honors, most of them daughters of noble or gentry lords with little prospects of advancement except through advantageous marriages. This was not the world Sirie had imagined would be waiting for them but Sirie was ahead of her time and so was Rowena. The princess christened her new band of warriors, fifteen in total at its inception, The Sisters of War.

* * * * *

Now, she was walking through a siege camp where she had been brought in, along with her band of warriors, to provide much need logistical support. This meant simply that they were to help load wagons, haul supplies, such as stones for the trebuchets, oil and pitch for breaching the doors or water for the tired soldiers. Sirie had always emphasized that no work on the battlefield was trivial but this felt like the work of children, not skilled warriors.

Rowena looked around and to her left she saw the commanders of the sieging army, sitting around a fire near their tents. They were laughing and drinking. She counted several other mercenary captains in the mix but she was not welcomed among them. She was a woman and women only had one role on the battlefield; carry water.

"Fuck this." She said before walking off to where her band's tents were pitched. She found a few of her companions sitting around one fire and several were grumbling at the circumstances. Once Rowena arrived they all rose to attention. "Our contract ends at dawn. They will ask us to stay on I'm sure. You all can do whatever the hell you want but I'm riding out tonight. Anyone not wishing to put up with being second rate gleaners are welcome to join me."

"Captain, I understand the desire to not sign up again but leaving tonight?" One of the women said. She was new to her command, not one of the original graduates, but Rowena recognized her as Selwyn Ashe's granddaughter, Morgana. She was young and a recent graduate, still learning the art of war and the truths of being a warrior.

Rowena nodded. "We've been paid in full and that's their loss because our skills have been wasted. I've been silent because they paid us our due so I'm cutting my losses and leaving for the next job. I imagine more than a few will ride with me but I'm not going to take any that don't wish to go."

"We'll all go with ye cap'n." Elva, the second in command and Rowena's oldest friend said. The statuesque woman was a member of the famed Hardstone Family, an easy thing to figure out given her stature and accent. "Ye know that, but I am wondering why we're sneaking off in the night?"

Rowena nodded. It was a valid question given her reputation as an honorable soldier. "Once we refuse to sign on it is entirely possible that this whole camp could turn on us and we're fifty eight against nearly ten thousand. I'm all up for a challenge but that's beyond our capabilities."

The other women nodded in agreement. Elva turned to the others. "Pack up quietly and be quick about it. Pass the word to our sisters that are sleeping." She said before kicking dirt on the fire to snuff it out.

The warriors worked quickly and a few hours before dawn, the mercenary band rode away from the siege camp. Being in the back of the camp has its advantages sometimes. True to Elva's words the entire mercenary band left the camp with Rowena. While she wasn't extremely surprised, she knew that her open door policy allowed for the warriors to make their own decisions. This was part of why her warriors loved her. Rowena knew what it was like to be shunned thus she allowed her warriors a voice of their own. Contrary to her mercenary captain counterparts, she wasn't a brutish type person. Her smile was pleasant and warm, like her father's and like him, she was kind to others. It was no wonder that her band was so loyal. It was also little wonder that she had suitors should she choose to settle down and become a nobleman's wife. However, that is not who she wanted to be at this point.

The sun was high in the sky when the group rode up to a roadside inn nearly fifteen miles away from the siege. The occupants, not many to be honest, did not seem to be bothered in the least by the war not far from them.

"Less than a day's ride and these people drink their lives away." Severa, daughter of Baron Harbor said as she and a few others tied up the horses. "Back home these people would be conscripted."

"Maybe by your father but not by the king." Another woman, Matilda, spoke up. "Now back to the horses and don't let the captain hear you lollygagging." Matilda was strict with the new recruits and fiercely loyal to Rowena. Many were and from the outside it might look like it was because she was a princess, but it truth it was deeper than that.

Rowena for her part never made anyone acknowledge her as a princess but as their captain, that much was evident. She also made sure everyone knew that noble standing was irreverent. In Lotcala, these warriors would have led different lives. Lives more accustomed to their blood status but as long as they rode with Rowena they lived a harder yet more rewarding life. In truth, they stayed out of Lotcala as much as possible. In Lotcala, the band of warriors were respected but they were not hired as much. Mostly, Rowena believed, that was because people were afraid of working with the king's daughter. Whatever the case was, she traveled further out into foreign lands, partially for the adventure she sought in her youth but also because there were more opportunity.

As Rowena and a few others settled down to a table the talk turned back to the previous job.

"I knew we couldn't trust those damn freeholders! They're always fighting for towns and settlements. Give them a year and we'll be hearing calls for another one trying to take some town." Ingrid Hafmen, daughter to the Manor Lord of Hafmen, said aloud. Ingrid had been a classmate of Rowena's and was another of her oldest friends. Ingrid continued as a server brought some trays of food and ale. "I can take gleaning a battlefield if it meant that something beneficial would be gained. Holding the land for a year or two isn't worth the lives lost."

Rowena lifted her tankard of ale as if in a toast. "We need a true lord to sign on to." She remarked before drinking the sweet, brown ale.

Elva emptied in one gulp as was usual for the tough woman, slamming the tankard down on the table. "We could head north. Plenty of fighting in the north."

"There aren't any wars going on currently in the north. Unless you plan to fight simple bandit raids for low pay then that's not really going to work out." Grainne Cullenhun replied with a smile. Grainne was the quartermaster of the group and handled the money that went to the sisters, as well as lining up new jobs. "After I eat I'll start asking around for some leads."

As more of the mercenary band filtered into the inn the server began to take notice of who was sitting where. She looked around as she carried the food and water, finally she walked back to the first table. The server had deduced that this was the table where the leader sat.

The woman, wearing a dirty dress and looking disheveled by the increased workload, walked over and looked at Grainne. "Miss, if I could have a moment of your time. We are in dire need. There have been killings and mutilations not far from here. A group of rebels have been coming and stalking the residents of the community as of late."

The four women at the table smiled. Grainne looked to the server. "And you think me the leader of this merry band of women?" she said with a grin, leaning back into her chair, crossing her legs.

"Aye miss. You seem to be the one everyone speaks about, the woman mercenary leader."

Grainne turned to Rowena and grinned widely. "You hear that captain?"

The server stifled a gasp once she looked to Rowena.

Rowena chuckled and nodded. She was used to the reaction after a few years on the road. She looked human enough but she had a few dwarven features. She was shorter than the average human woman, standing only four feet and nine inches tall and built rather stocky, much more like a dwarf than a human but it should be noted that her father was not a lean man, rather more muscular. Her hair was a dark red and this gave her face a darker frame. When looking at the woman compared to her closest companions, it was easy to overlook her. Her most noticeable feature was that on the right side of her face was a long scar from her forehead to her chin, given to her by another warrior's blade in the Southern Kingdoms.

"The dwarf?" The server questioned with scrunched up nose. In the southern regions, dwarves were discriminated against more so than the north.

"A bit o' respect for our Captain Rowena if ye please." Elva remarked, grabbing the hilt of her sword making her intentions known to the server. Other women close by stood up to look on.

The server began to frantically apologize. "Forgive me please. I was unaware and I assumed..."

Rowena held up her hand to stop her stuttering and to let her warriors know to settle down. "That's fine." Rowena said, letting the woman's insult go. "I guess some stories don't include my appearance." Rowena smiled as the server grew flustered. "Let's talk about these rebels instead."

"Umm...yes of course." The server wrung a cloth in her hands. "You see..."

"Bah! Sit down lass, me neck is getting sore looking up at ye!" Elva said, pulling the woman a chair from the next table.

"Thank you." The server replied, sitting down. "They have been ravaging livestock and then they killed several residents in recent days since that last battle. They stayed behind when everyone else moved onto the castle. They carry a red banner with a black horse on it. Whenever our villagers see it we run and hide. We need help."

Rowena looked to her companions. "Sounds like that bastard Forkbeard." The others nodded grimly. "He and his men were exiled by the lord early on during the siege. I figured they'd head to the other army and join up against us but I guess not."

Elva looked to Rowena. "That's a bit o' trouble then. Forkbeard is King Rutger's bastard."

Rowena chuckled while the others at the table and a few at a table close by eyed the scene with great intent. "And I'm the King of Lotcala's bastard."

"Aye ye are but I'd never call ye that." Elva smirked.

Rowena returned the smile to her best friend and then looked to the server. "Forkbeard is a slimy piece of dung and he undercut us a few jobs back. We might be interested."

Ingrid smirked. "He's competition. Folks will say that you're fighting the competition just to get rid of them."

Rowena nodded to her friend. "Normally I'd agree with you but he has sunk to pillaging this village and the surrounding roads. Besides, I have mouths to feed, warriors and horses to take care of and company provisions to think about, none of which is cheap." Rowena looked back to the server. "What can you offer?"

"Room and board, free." The woman replied.

"That's a start." Rowena replied stoically. She was known as a brave woman but she was shrewd. Her band of sisters needed coin to survive.

"A start?" The server stammered. "What more could a dwar..."

"Gold and or silver my dear." Grainne responded, cutting the server off before she insulted Rowena again.

"We don't have much." The woman said.

"Gather what you have and then we'll finish the conversation." Grainne smiled. The server nodded and began to get up to leave. Grainne caught her by the wrist. "Best to check with the other villagers too." She then let go of the woman and turned back to the table. "We won't get rich off this one."

"No, but with Forkbeard out of the picture we might get more jobs in the future." Ingrid replied. "That excuse for human gives us mercs a bad name."

"True but he gets results." Grainne replied. She sipped her ale. "And he makes a fortune, though some of his gains are off of his pillaging."

As night fell, the group left the inn and ventured out into the darkness. A small band of five broke off and rode slowly down a secluded forest road while the rest of the mercenaries stalked behind, from the tree line.

Rowena led those five women down the dark path. On her horse she slowly trotted along. The others behind her kept their eyes peeled, ever vigilant, into the darkness of the forest. The air was still and the wind wafted softly around them but nothing seemed to be amiss. For all intents and purposes, this was a normal night. Rowena cursed her luck and turned her horse.

"To the inn." She said, leading her party and those off the sides back to the inn and their camp. "We'll search for tracks in the morning." Elva, next to her on one side and Ingrid was on the other. Two novice mercenaries flanked them. Rowena, Elva and Ingrid stopped short as the other two rode a few more steps before looking back. Rowena looked out. Something had caught her attention. A familiar sound, a twang in the stillness of the night. More than a few twangs rang out alerting the band to the coming danger.

"Ride!" Rowena ordered. The group turned just as a barrage of arrows rained down from the sky. One of the novice mercenaries with her was hit by multiple arrows and dropped from her horse. Rowena and the other three women stopped in their tracks as they heard the war cries from beyond the trees.

Rowena's mercenaries burst from the trees, some on horseback while others were fighting on foot. A few more took arrow wounds but Forkbeard's men entered the battle from the other side of the path and engaged against the women warriors.

Both sides clashed in a violent and bloody show. Rowena dismounted and drew her longsword from its sheath on her side, charging into the battle lines that had formed. She brought the blade down in a hacking motion on top of an opponent, severing his shoulder in two. Others were faring better while some of her mercenaries were not. She saw warriors fall to sword strikes and even a few more to arrows.

Quickly Rowena turned and blocked an axe blow before kicking the wielder back and stabbing him in his belly with a thrust of her sword.

Rowena stepped back from the battle. "Go now to the inn and take up a defense!" Rowena ordered to Elva.

"Aye!" Elva replied, calling out as she rode with the others calling for the rest of the warriors to fallback.

Rowena rushed to her fallen comrade and hoisted her up and onto her horse nearby. Many of her soldiers were providing cover and soon they were off and out of arrow range. She noted on the way back to the inn that Forkbeard's men did not give chase.

She found the inn guarded, wagons and barrels over turned, with her soldiers ready with bows out, arrows nocked. She got off her horse and as gently as she could, given her haste, she pulled the other woman off the horse.

Grainne rushed over to help her. "What happened out there?" She asked as they rushed into the inn. Finding a table, they laid the woman there but by then it was too late.

Rowena looked down at the dead soldier. "They set an ambush." Rowena looked around. "Anyone else hurt?"

Grainne looked solemn. "Two others dead from arrows. We left them where they fell but besides them we're missing four others that haven't returned. There have been a few come back with other wounds, sword and spear, and I'm afraid one or two might not make it through the night. Ingrid is tending to a couple of the wounded. We'll return for the dead in the morning."

"Guard the inn and send the wounded that can still hold a bow out to the fortifications. We'll need all the able bodied out there. Forkbeard can bring over a hundred men to a battle on any given day and an attack like that shows we're outnumbered." Rowena said, walking away from the dead soldier.

Grainne simply nodded before walking back out to the grounds.

* * * * *

Rowena sat by the fire of the inn and stared into the flame. She thought back to her youth and the days in the War Academy. She hated being stuck but a large group such as hers would attract attention. After a few minutes she went out to the defenses and waited with her sisters but dawn rose with little fanfare or incident.

"He's out there." Elva said, looking to the forest line. "He's waiting."

"Yeah, he is." Rowena replied stoically.

"I say let's go and find him." Elva responded, looking to her captain.

"We're far outnumbered. At least staying here he has to fight against us and our defenses." Rowena said.

"What defenses?!" Elva shout back angrily. "A couple up turned wagons and some crates on the ground?" She threw her hands up. "We've done better cap'n!"

Rowena stepped up to the larger Elva, standing over a foot taller than the captain. "I rather not get any more of my sisters killed!" The captain glared up at her second in command. She might have been smaller but her temper, when provoked, was larger than life. "Now stand down Elva."

Elva snorted and sneered. She was a Hardstone and that meant she didn't like being bossed around or being at a disadvantage. However, being a Hardstone meant she was loyal and knew how to follow orders. They were born soldiers and Elva was no different.

"Aye cap'n." Elva said, stepping back.

Rowena looked to the crowd gathered and to the others watching from nearby. "We'll beat Forkbeard and his lot, but it will take more than strength. We will need something of a plan." She looked to Elva. "Besides a pitch battle and guerilla tactics, does anyone have a suggestion?"

Severa stepped up. "We could leave." Others around the woman began to react with anger and even Rowena scowled but Severa put her hands up, asking the others to wait. "A ruse. We leave and then let them think we're pulling out of here, defeated, but then we flank and rout them."

"A gamble at best." Ingrid responded. "But there aren't many other options apart from being walled up here."

"What choice do we have?" Severa responded.

"We can barter with him." Rowena said stoically. The others looked to their captain, confused by the notion. Rowena caught on to their cues. "You'll see." Rowena then walked inside the inn and retrieved a white cloth. She returned and went to her horse. "Stay here until I return or until nightfall. After that leave." Before long Rowena was riding off, down the dirt path and into the forest.

Everyone sat and waited in anticipation. Grainne was the first to react. "She's been gone too long. What the hell do you think she was planning?"

"Who knows but I wouldn't trust that damn Forkbeard with a grain of sand." Ingrid answered.

Just then a sentry called out to the others that Rowena was returning.

The captain dismounted and went to a pail with water. She took the ladle and drank a large gulp.

"Captain? What happened?" Severa asked.

"I challenged him to a duel. If he wins, then we, more than likely you all, will leave and leave him to his pillaging. If I win then he leaves with all his warriors."

"Yer expecting him to honor his pledge?" Elva asked skeptically.

Rowena shook her head. "No, I'm not. I'm also not expecting to lose. His men will see me defeat him and some will lose heart in him and leave, others may react differently."

"Differently?" Grainne wondered aloud.

"They'll try to fight." Rowena answered. "Kill them. Arrows should do the trick. Be warned that most of his men and starving and they might be desperate. Be prepared for a possible fight."

"Forgive me cap'n, but yer certain ye can beat him?" Elva asked.

Rowena looked to Elva and her face grew grim. "We'll find out at first light."

* * * * *

The band of sisters kept their nighttime guard as the forests beyond were eerily still. Inside the inn Rowena sat near a roaring hearth. She warmed her hands by the fire and barely moved when the server reappeared with a sack full of gold, silver and valuables.

"It's all we have ma'am." She said in a meek voice. "We scrounged up every crown piece we could find."

Rowena looked up to the woman and motioned for her to lay the bag on the floor before turning back to the fire. The woman complied and began to turn but stopped short.

"Ma'am? May I ask you a question?"

Rowena looked back to the woman. She was sullen and tired but still Rowena had to admire the resilience left in her and the rest of the village.

"What is it?" Rowena inquired, trying not to sound too gruff.

"When did you stop being afraid of people like…him?"

Rowena smirked. "People like Forkbeard?" She chuckled. "I was nearly ten when I stopped being afraid. That was the first time I killed a man. An assassin trying to kill my father."

"And then you became a mercenary?" The woman asked.

Rowena shook her head. "No. Then I was trained some more before being sent to an old, abandoned castle that my stepmother took over and I was trained even more. Some of these women here now were with me even back then. After that I became a mercenary."

"And you're not like him? Going town to town and charging for your skills." The woman raised an eyebrow.

"I try not to be. Forkbeard has turned to robbing and pillaging. We fight for gold the same but we don't steal it. However, we do have to charge for our service."

The woman gave a small sneer, not understanding the difference. "He 'offered' to protect us for a large fee but not as large as the fee that I've just dropped at your muddy dwarf feet."

Rowena stood up at the utter of the word 'dwarf'. Rowena hated to be called a dwarf. She wasn't quite as tall as the woman but only a couple inches shorter. "Then you should have taken his offer."

The woman looked down on Rowena. "You and your band have a job to do and then we expect you to leave. You've overstayed your welcome." The woman said before turning to walk off.

"Hey, wench!" Rowena stood up and called to the woman, who turned around startled. "Always remember that you will sometimes be the bad guy in someone's story. The choice is then up to you in determining how true that really is. My loyalties are to my sisters, my father, my brothers and their mother; my family. My loyalties, our loyalties, to you end once this gold is spent."

Rowena stood in the dimly lit room, watching the server walk out of the room without saying a word. It seemed many jobs lately were turning sour for Rowena's band. The captain shrugged, she'd put up with it as long as they got paid well enough.

The next morning Rowena walked out of the inn and into the yard outside. She had donned her chainmail over padded cloth and her nasal helm. Over her mail she wore a leather vest with her personal coat of arms, a ship under five gold coins on a green field. She was flanked by her soldiers as she approached Forkbeard and his soldiers. Many looked as starved and desperate as Rowena had described them. Forkbeard, however, looked rested, fit and strong.

"Finally you come out of that run down shit hole!" Forkbeard taunted.

Rowena turned to Elva. "If he tries to double-cross us then fill him and anyone you can with arrows."

"Aye cap'n."

Forkbeard laughed. His larger stomach protruded from under his gambeson and his blond beard covered much of the lower half of his face. "There'll be no need for that. My men will act with honor. Can you say the same for your wenches there behind you?"

"With your example I would not stake my life on your men being honorable but my sisters will respect the pledge I made in good faith." Rowena retorted. She then pulled her sword from its sheath and grabbed her shield. "Time to end this."

Forkbeard smiled and grabbed his sword, a larger and thicker blade than Rowena's leaf blade sword. The two combatants moved toward each other, the warriors from around the fighters circled them into the makeshift arena. Rowena took the chance for the first strike and swung wide. Forkbeard dodged out of the way.

"With your fat belly I had thought I'd hit something." Rowena taunted with a smirk.

The joke did not go over all too well with the larger warrior. "I'll gut you dwarf!" Forkbeard replied angrily. He then lunged into an attack and brought his sword down hard but Rowena lifted her shield in time to deflect the blow.

The warrior woman pushed hard with her shield and knocked the bigger man back, bringing a cheer from Rowena's band. She then tried to hack at him with her own sword swing but Forkbeard was able to roll out of the way. Rowena's sword slashed into the dirt but she rebounded quickly. Forkbeard tried to swing on Rowena but in her rebound she was able to parry his swing. Forkbeard swung again and Rowena lifted her shield to deflect his blow.

However, it was a mighty blow from the large warrior. Rowena held her shield up to absorb the force but her left knee buckled and she dropped to the ground. The crowd cheering for Forkbeard exclaimed out in joy at their captain's success. Rowena held fast onto her shield but she felt her strength wane.

Rowena's mind raced as she thought to the man pushing down on her shield and her warrior sisters watching on. She thought back to her training and to the days with Sirie, being pushed to the breaking point, day in and day out. The years of torment with a woman that despised her but still cared enough to teach her everything she knew. Rowena thought to the pain of her youth and what it meant to show the rest of the world that she belonged.

With a mighty roar she pushed back and kicked out at Forkbeard's knee, dropping the larger man to the ground again. This time she was quicker and she pounced on the warrior with all of her strength. She drove her shield onto Forkbeard's chest and even under the heavy padding he felt the brunt force, with a few ribs cracking from the pressure. Rowena dropped her sword and reared back before punching the man's face, square on his nose. She continued to pommel him with punches and then finally she smashed her helmeted head into his face, caving in his nasal cavity and skull.

Rowena lifted herself off of the fallen mercenary leader and for good measure she took her sword and slit Forkbeard's throat. His men began to grumble and shout but Elva and the other Sisters raised their bows and aimed arrows at the angry men.

Rowena stood up and lifted a hand into the air. "I beat him fairly and by the rules of the challenge. Be proud knowing that he fought hard." She panted. "But nonetheless he fell and I am the victor. Go now and fulfill the pledge hard won."

The scene was tense but most nodded and went off as agreed. A few stragglers stayed behind but they too eventually wondered off and away from the village.

Rowena and her band of warriors watched them leave and she stood for a few moments after. Elva approached her captain and clasped her on the shoulder.

"It's done then, eh?"

Rowena looked up to Elva. "Yeah, we're done." The two smiled. "You think we'll ever settle down from this life and find husbands, have a family and live in peace?"

Elva laughed. "Ain't a man alive that handle us lass!"

Rowena joined in the laughter as did a few others. They finally turned back and began to pack up their horses. Grainne grabbed the sack of gold and silver, loading it onto a horse for the journey. She'd divide it up later, for now they all knew the plan was to leave with haste and to find their next adventure.

Grainne looked to the other women as they began to ride off. "I heard talk of a beast problem twenty miles or so east of here. Maybe we could get some coin from hunting wild game?"

Rowena smiled. "East it is!"

There be Dragons!

"My grandmother slayed a dragon when she was in her twenty fifth year!" This brought laughs from the people gathered in the great hall of the court of Ceasarn, a large hold on the southern tip of the central Continent. "She did!" Gisela exclaimed. "She also conquered the lands to the west and made them her own." It was then that the court stopped laughing at the young woman in loose fitting chainmail and leather. "Oh, now you'll listen?"

"Are you speaking of Queen Rowena the Dauntless?" the lord of the hall exclaimed.

The young woman beamed with pride. "I am indeed!" She lifted her head, her dark brown hair falling below her shoulders. "I am her granddaughter, Princess Gisela of the Kingdom of Nashoba, Land of the Wolves!"

The crowd began to gasp and murmur for it wasn't often that a royal from Nashoba ventured away from the large kingdom. Queen Caribe had never stepped foot out of Nashoba and neither had her other daughters or her son. This was an auspicious occasion to say the least. Rowena had conquered Nashoba in her fifties and she spent twenty years bringing the kingdom to heel, so much so that her daughter thought it prudent to remain close in case of trouble. Rowena's grandchildren did the same; all except one, Gisela. A stubborn and unruly girl of eighteen but gifted with a fearless attitude.

"Rumors are swirling that say you are having trouble with a dragon. I came to slay the beast!" Gisela continued.

"Forgive me young one." An older gentleman to the right of the lord began. "But most dragon slayers are older, bigger and stronger men."

"And dead!" The lord said in a booming voice. "There haven't been any dragon slayers since the Dragonsbanes died out nearly a century ago, besides it was a century prior to that since the last dragon was spotted."

"Then what the hell torched that town at the border?" Gisela asked raising an eyebrow.

"A band of lawless mercs. Similar to what your grandmother used to lead." The lord replied.

Gisela smiled at the supposed insult. She knew the truth and the pride behind her grandmother's past. "Then what harm will it be for me to investigate?"

"Harm?" The lord questioned excitedly. "If something happens to you then your mother brings a host of warriors down on my city! No! Be gone with you and your fanciful tales of mythical beasts! There's nothing but brigands and ruffians anyway."

Just then the court door swung open with a loud bang and a messenger ran it.

"Dragon! A dragon just burned a farming village north of here and it flew this way! Run!"

Gisela smiled at the lord. "What harm will it be for me to look into this and maybe receive twenty pounds of silver and ten pounds of rubies?"

The lord slunk back into his throne and dropped his head into his hand. "Fine." He said, leaving Gisela to smile and turn off as she left the court.

The crowds outside of the castle were clamoring for anything they could carry as news of the dragon had spread like a swarm of locusts on crops. Gisela walked into a nearby tavern, one she heard was popular with adventurers and mercenaries.

Gisela burst through the doors, shield and spear strapped to her back and her nasal helm under cradled her arm.

"I'm looking for some hearty folks to share in an adventure! Dragon slaying!" She called out with a grin stretching ear to ear.

In the tavern, dimly lit and smelling of beer and piss, not a soul moved. Gisela was undeterred.

"There is gold and gems in it for whomever travels with me and lives!" She exclaimed but again no one even turned her way. "So I take it this lot is a bunch of cowards pretending to be men? No balls in the whole place!"

That sparked the tavern patrons as they all turned to regard her. A large burly man, nearly seven foot tall and built like two men, stood up and walked to her. "Tough walk from a short and thin whelp of a girl. It wouldn't take much to teach you some manners."

The large man lunged at Gisela but she was quick as she tossed her helm in his face and then dropped low. She turned her leg with speed and swept the big man off his feet, he landed with a thud onto the wooden floor. While still propped up by her palms on the floor, Gisela lifted her right leg and then dropped it down on the man's groin. The would be 'manners instructor' cried out in pain and coughed up blood in a large gulp.

Gisela hopped up and picked up her helm. "I honestly did not think that would hurt you, given that I thought you were nutless." Gisela shrugged. "So does anyone want to go and seek glory and riches? Dragon hides are excellent for making armor." Most just turned back to their drinks.

An old man sitting at the bar turned around, probably the only man that didn't bother looking earlier during the ruckus, and eyed the young woman. "Why would you want to go kill a dragon? Dangerous business dragons. Live your life, get married and have babies. That's the best a woman can hope for, besides you're what, sixteen?"

Gisela scoffed. "I'm nineteen you wrinkly son of a bitch! I don't want to get married and have babies, I'm wanting adventure like my grandmother had! I'm Gisela of Nashoba, granddaughter of the great Queen Rowena!"

"And?" The old man shrugged.

"And?" Gisela exclaimed. "And I want to kill a damn dragon and seek my glory!"

The old man chuckled. "Rowena wanted to seek glory too and she got half her sisters killed because of it."

Gisela walked closer to the old man's seat. "I know the tale." Gisela said with clinched teeth. "Maybe I want to do it a bit differently."

"I don't really care but you've interrupted our drinking so if me giving you a tip is what gets you out of here then so be it." The old man stood up and pointed to his left. "Head down that road and about two miles down there will be a small shack a few hundred yards off the road. There you'll find a knight named Vincent. He might help you but no one here wants any part of that beast." The old man turned back to the bar.

Gisela nodded. "Fine then and thanks." She turned and left, stepping on the large man's stomach as she walked over him. "Oops." She said.

Following the old man's advice, Gisela rode up to the shack and found a shabbily dressed man chopping fire wood.

"Are you Sir Vincent?" She asked.

The man looked up to Gisela. "Depends?"

"On?"

"Are you're the crazy girl hunting dragons that don't exist?" the man replied.

"No, I'm the crazy girl that is actually a full grown woman hunting dragons that are burning villages. If you're Sir Vincent then speak up or let me be on my way."

The man returned to chopping his logs. Gisela gave an hmpf and turned to ride off. "It'll smell you coming."

"Excuse me?" Gisela said, turning back to Vincent.

"The dragon will smell you. You smell like wealth. Dragons like that." Vincent stood up straight from his chopping and leaned his axe against the stomp. "Have you ever even walked onto a battlefield because I'd guess you haven't?"

"Well...I..."

Vincent snorted. "Figured." He picked up his axe. "Why not go back home and live comfortably?" He picked up a log and positioned it on the stomp.

"Because my brother will be king and my sister will lead his army. I'll be left with nothing unless I make my own way. I've been trained and I can fight."

"Of that I have no doubt. They say you are the granddaughter of Rowena the Apostate."

"The Dauntless." Gisela corrected.

"The Cruel." Vincent responded.

Gisela stiffened. "The Conqueror."

"The Dwarven Bastard." Vincent chided.

Gisela scowled at the man. "You must want my blade to separate your head from your neck."

Vincent looked back up and smiled. "Nope, just testing you. Your grandmother was a hell of a woman but she was all those things. Accept it."

"Why is it that everywhere I go, I'm judged by her?"

"Because that's your only claim to fame at this point. So we hunt a dragon and then what?"

Gisela's face softened. "It's a simple plan really; kill the dragon then come back for the reward. We live off the coin and gems and probably drink until we fuck and then go our separate ways."

"All that sounds good except that you're not really my type. I prefer another persuasion." Vincent replied with a grin.

"To the point. I like that." Gisela smiled knowingly. She dismounted and approached the man. "It'll be just the two of us so that silver and those gems will be split down the middle, if we live." She made a notion with her hands indicating a fifty/fifty split.

"What makes you think that I'm agreeing to this insanity?"

Gisela lowered her head and then turned to look off to her left. "That grave is marked with the Dragonbane crest. Family, friend or lover?"

"Husband." Vincent said looking to the grave as well. "We were Dragonsbanes. We were the last of our kind. Now I'm the last."

"And yet everyone thinks the Dragonsbanes were killed off years ago?"

"Most of us were but a handful lived through the purge, trying to recruit and build the order again but we failed and now I'm the last. Dragonsbane is still a mark of death in some nations, fearful of what we might be capable of and fearful that more lived."

Gisela looked to Vincent. "Did more live?"

"No."

There was a solemn silence between the pair before Gisela decided that enough time had passed for respectful mourning. "So, at dawn we ride out?" Gisela asked.

"If you say so." Vincent replied. He helped stable her horse and walked her inside.

The next morning the pair, both clad in chainmail armor and leather, rode off toward the northern plains to find their prey.

The pair rode through the day and as dusk neared they came upon the first burnt village.

"The lord had said this was bandits." Gisela remarked as they trotting along.

"Bandits can't set a fire that will melt stone." Vincent replied.

"Liquid fire?"

Vincent shook his head. "Liquid fire leaves a rotten smell. These planks," he said pointing to some burnt wood, "they're still smoldering but there isn't a hint of sulfur. The only other thing that can melt stone but not leave a sulfur smell for days is dragon's breath."

"Then the hunt is on." Gisela smiled.

Vincent dismounted and crouched on the ground. "Here are some tracks. Small for a dragon."

"Young?"

Vincent nodded. "A baby."

Gisela frowned. "Not much glory in hunting and killing a baby dragon but the reward's the same."

"I hate killing baby dragons." Vincent scowled. "If the dragon is a major threat, baby or not then we would do whatever is necessary. You rarely find a baby without a mother. That's the danger of finding a baby. A mother dragon is more dangerous than any other dragon."

"An adult dragon, now there's the glory! So do we follow the tracks?"

Vincent rolled his eyes. "That would be my suggestion."

They rode off, following the tracks. The ride, deeper into the hills at the foot of the mountains, gave them the opportunity to talk a more openly.

"How was your grandmother in private?" Vincent asked.

"What do you mean?" Gisela skewed her eyes. "She was a typical grandmother; milk, pastries and gifts every time we saw her."

"Really?"

"Hell no!" Gisela laughed. "She was cold and distant unless…"

"Unless what?" Vincent questioned at Gisela's pause.

Gisela sighed. "Unless you proved your worth in her eyes. For the most part she was void of any emotions. Her stepmother saw to that. She ripped all of that out of her at every chance and it tormented her but once she left Lotcala she became her own woman."

"There are a lot of stories about her and her mercenary band. A brave and fearsome bunch."

"Yeah and we heard them all growing up, even the ones about the abuse from her stepmother. Still, her stories of all her battles were my favorites. Some big boots to fill, you know." Gisela smiled. "Even when you go back further to the ancestors. Long line of big ass boots."

"Have you ever been to Lotcala?" Vincent asked.

"Nah. Grandmother made sure to make it known that we weren't welcome there. After her father Charles died, Sirie put a bounty on her head and then her brother did as well once. Too bad for them all those assassins never got the job done." Gisela smirked.

"She was an amazing warrior." Vincent smiled to Gisela.

Gisela returned the smile. "Better than that bitch Sirie." Gisela turned back to the path they were walking. "One day I want to go to Lotcala and meet their king and tell him that we don't want his worthless kingdom. Then I'll turn around so he can kiss my ass before I walk out of his hall."

Vincent laughed. "From the stories they tell, you are every bit your grandmother. What about you and your family now? Bounties I mean?"

"You wish to collect?" Gisela looked over to Vincent but the man just shook his head. "Yeah, they want us dead too. Dead people can't claim thrones. A group of assassins came a few years back and my mother and father put their heads on ship and sent it up north to Lotcala. They even wrote a nice little letter to the king to leave us alone unless he wants the next ship to be accompanied by the royal fleet. Since then it's been quiet."

Vincent laughed for a moment, Gisela joined him, but then Vincent went silent. "Shh!"

Gisela looked over. "What is it? Do you see something?"

Vincent pointed to a cave nearly two hundred yards away in the foothills. "There. That cave looks like a dragon's lair."

Gisela put her hand above her eyes to block the sun for better vision. "How can you tell from this distance?"

"Trained to spot the signs but the most obvious sign is the trail of cow remains and large claw marks on the sides of the cave entrance."

"Okay, I get the remains but damn, how can you see the claw marks from this far away?"

"I have good vision. Let's go." Vincent replied.

They galloped to the cave and dismounted just to the south, out of the wind. After tying their horses to a tree, the pair pulled their weapons and readied themselves. Gisela had her grandmother's spear and a round shield while Vincent only had his Dragonsbane spear and sword, though the sword was sheathed.

He whispered to Gisela. "Be quiet and walk slowly, stay vigilant." Gisela nodded.

They crept through the cave, finding the remains of many farm animals along the way and even some bones from the wild beasts around the area. However, both warriors noticed the strange absence of human remains.

"Normally we would be seeing more than just animals." Vincent said.

"That makes since but no human remains means what?"

Vincent wasn't sure how to answer that. "Even babies would take humans, mostly children or smaller adults, but they don't differentiate between different types of meat."

Gisela nodded. "Then let's find this beast before it figures that out."

They walked deeper into the cave, as the sun light faded Gisela went to one knee and took an old cloth from her pouch and a flint. She wrapped the cloth on a femur bone of a large animal and then struck a rock with the flint a few times to spark the cloth. It wasn't as good as a normal torch but it was good enough to light their way. She would be without her shield though. It was of little comfort at best against dragon's breath and the torch was more useful. The cave was pitch black and damp, water dripped from stalactites and roots from above ground trees poked through the roof of the cave.

After a few moments of walking in the darkness the pair could hear the soft sound of a dragon breathing.

"It's close." Vincent whispered. He took the lead and soon they came upon the sleeping beast, already over twelve feet long and Vincent figured it weighed over a ton.

"We can end this now and then take its head for the reward." Gisela said. Vincent nodded and both got ready to strike. Gisela put the torch down and grabbed her spear with both heads. They poised themselves and inched in to strike but just as they were raising their spears a voice shook them from behind.

"Stop!"

"What?!" Vincent and Gisela both said. The dragon stirred but it did not wake up completely.

They turned and saw a figure standing there. They peered through the darkness and tried to make out the shape of the figure. They saw a feminine form but there was something unusual about her head. They could see something moving around it.

"Umm...hello." The silhouette said meekly as it waved awkwardly. "I'm Agota. I'm the dragon's mother, well sort of."

"Dragon's mother?" Vincent asked in disbelief.

"Sort of?" Gisela asked. Both lowered their spears slightly.

Agota stepped closer to the torch and they could see the beautiful woman with a sweet smile come to view, a beautiful woman with snakes wrapping around her head.

"You're a gorgon!" Gisela shouted raising her spear and closing her eyes.

Behind her the dragon shot up and roared. Though it was a baby, it had a piercing cry. Gisela turned around and brought her spear up in defense. Agota rushed passed by them and put her hands on the dragon's neck and body.

"Shh. It's okay. I won't let them hurt you." Agota comforted. "Please don't hurt him. He's just a baby and I'm teaching him not to be threat to humans." She said turning her head to the warriors.

"What do you mean teaching him?" Vincent asked, looking at the ground.

Agota was getting the dragon to fall back asleep, rubbing his neck and humming a soft tune. "Please just head to the entrance of the cave and I'll meet you there once Egis is asleep."

"Egis?" Gisela questioned.

"The dragon." Agota clarified.

"Fine but no tricks." Vincent replied with an authoritative voice.

"Like you'd be able to stop me." Agota snapped. "Now go."

Vincent and Gisela did as requested and a few moments later the heard Agota walking up. Both shielded their eyes.

"You can uncover your eyes. I'm not going to turn you into stone." Agota chuckled. She knelt down over a smoldered fire and added some wood and kindling before striking a flint to get the fire started again. In the light of the fire they could see the woman better. She looked around the same age as Gisela and she wore brown leather pants, boots and a cloth shirt. Gisela and Vincent could both see small wings coming from her back. Atop her head were snakes, with green and purple scales similar to Agota's own skin, slithering around, they did not look menacing though. Agota looked up and saw both Vincent and Gisela still covering their eyes. "I won't turn you into stone. Not unless you try to attack me."

Gisela slowing lowered her shield. "What do you mean? You can control it?" She glanced to Vincent and saw him begin to peek with his left eye.

"Yes. I mean as a kid no but now as an adult I can. It's like venom from a snake. The mature snakes can control how much venom they pump into their prey but the babies can't. They just pump all they can. Same concept." Agota said, trying to smile. She had a beautiful smile and she did her best to set the two warriors at ease.

Gisela lowered her spear. "So you're not a threat?"

"No, are you?" Agota replied, raising an eyebrow in exhaustion.

"We come for the dragon, though." Gisela said.

Agota's eyes narrowed. "That's a Dragonsbane spear, are you one?" She asked, looking to Vincent. "I don't want to believe that you'll kill a baby." Her snakes perked up and hissed.

"I try not to." He gripped his spear tightly. "Not unless threatened or it threatens humans. Is it a threat to humans?"

Agota eyed the warrior. "Not as long as I finish training him."

"Training him?" Gisela asked.

Agota nodded. "I've trained a few of them in my time. All are friendly to humans; given the chance to prove it."

"Okay then if that's the case you have no quarrels with me. I'd rather not fight a gorgon to be honest, so I'll take you at your word." Vincent replied. "Besides I didn't want to kill a baby."

Agota nodded and then looked over to Gisela. "And what about you? Who are you two anyway?"

"I'm Gisela and this is Vincent." Gisela dropped her spear to her waist and lowered her shield. She felt defeated. "I just wanted to claim some sort of glory. The same my grandmother had or at least part of it. Maybe to get some gold too." She let out a soft laugh and shook her head. "We'll head on and leave you be."

"Your grandmother?"

Gisela straightened up. "Queen Rowena the Dauntless of –"

"Nashoba." Agota finished. Gisela smiled. "I thought I recognized that shield and spear. I met her and even journeyed with her for a time."

"Really?" Both Vincent and Gisela replied in shock.

Agota smiled. "I considered her a friend. I was young and just before she conquered Nashoba she took me in for a couple years. I was about fifteen and she saw me, took pity and allowed me to join her. Even trained me with a sword."

"Wow!" Gisela remarked with a large smile. She hadn't met many who had been trained by her grandmother, it all seemed unbelievable.

Agota smiled as well but it faded. "I was alone and starved. Winter time is a rough time in the mountains but she found me and over the many objections of her mercenary band she let me live. So many of my kind have been killed in fear but she didn't believe in killing an innocent gorgon. She had the right because, if I'm being honest, many of my kind, most of my kind, are not very friendly." She sniffed. "My mother and father were different and they taught me to be a friend to humans. Our whole village was friendly to humans but some warriors came through and..." Agota broke off, wiping away a tear. "I was hidden away but when I emerged I found everyone dead. I tried to make my way out and after a year, your grandmother found me and gave me a home."

"That doesn't sound like her, based on the stories." Vincent commented.

Gisela chuckled. "No it doesn't." She turned to the gorgon and narrowed her eyes. "It's a hell of a tale."

Agota nodded. "I know it's hard to believe but maybe this will give you some piece of mind." She took something from her pouch hanging at her side. "This was given to me by your grandmother years ago. She said to keep it safe and if anything ever were to happen to her that I was to open this and follow its instructions. She died a natural death so I left it unopened. Here."

Gisela took the letter and cracked its seal, her grandmother's seal. Her eyes widened as she read through the letter.

"What does it say?" Vincent asked.

"It's in my grandmother's handwriting. It just says that should anything happen to her to kill the ruler of Lotcala." She handed the letter to Vincent. "Signed by my grandmother."

"That it is." Vincent replied, reading over the letter before handing it back to Gisela.

"She trusted you enough to give you such an important task and secret. Not many people know the bad blood between her and Lotcala. This means something and you meant something to her. A confidant." Gisela remarked.

Agota smiled. "That, and I was a tool for vengeance against those that shunned and hunted her. I would have done it too but she lived a long and healthy life and then died peacefully. I did my best to keep up with news from the few contacts in the kingdom that had become friendly with me and I stayed close by too. Lots of dragons in this area anyway. Though the sacrifice is that I live in caves mostly and hide from towns. When I traveled with Rowena I was able to at least venture into town and hide the snakes." She motioned to her head. "I used an old shawl to wrap up my head. The snakes would go to sleep and then I could get a pint or two." Agota smiled.

"We'll keep your secret safe. We won't tell anyone you are here." Vincent said to reassure Agota.

"So then I guess that's it. We'll leave you and Egis in peace." Gisela said.

"Before you go let me give you something for a reward." She walked off to a tunnel off to the side and then came back with a large skull. "It's a giant's skull. Mountain giant to be exact. This was his cave. It was dead and so I claimed it and all the treasure."

"That skull would be worth a prize Gisela." Vincent said.

"Yea it would! Thank you." Gisela replied with a smile.

"It's the least I could do." Agota smiled. Behind the dragon lumbered up and dropped its head on Agota's shoulder.

Vincent and Gisela felt uneasy but smiled.

"I guess we'll have to figure something out about the burning villages." Vincent said.

Agota lightly tapped Egis on the nose. "He'll stay away. In fact maybe it's time to move away from this place. We can move somewhere without inhabitants."

"Why not come with me?" Gisela said. "I'll turn this skull in and then we can travel around and strike out on adventures. The four of us!" She finished, motioning to the dragon and Vincent.

"I don't know about that. The world might not be ready for us out there." Agota said with a frown.

"Yeah and I can't just leave my home." Vincent added.

"You mean that little shack?" Gisela chided.

Vincent sneered. "Some of us weren't born in castles."

"I'm sorry. I was thinking maybe you could get a fresh start. Adventure, creating new stories possibly new love. Maybe that's not the lifestyle for everyone but I think we could make a name for ourselves and even help dragons throughout the world." Gisela remarked.

"Okay, that sounds like it could be fun. I've been stuck in this cave for long enough and riding with Rowena's granddaughter would be an adventure, I'm sure." Agota smiled. "What say you Vincent?"

Vincent leaned on his spear. "Train friendly dragons? What would my ancestors say?"

"They'd say 'don't be an idiot and go with the gorgon and the princess!'" Gisela replied.

The knight lowered his head and grinned. "I would rather see mortal kind take a softer approach with some of the beasts of the world." Vincent replied. "I'm in."

Agota laughed, the snakes wrapping around her head slithered and moved rhythmically with her laugh. "You are nothing like your grandmother, Gisela." The remark brought a bit of a frown to Gisela. Agota smiled to the young woman. "You're funnier than her. She was a hard woman, a good woman but rough around the edges. Her husband though, now he was a joker. That's why they worked so well. You remind me of him."

"I never met him." Gisela confided.

"That's a shame. He was a good man and he loved your grandmother and she him." Agota gave Egis another pat. "Ahh, enough of this sentimental shit. Let's bundle up some of this gold and silver. I have some weapons over there that might be useful. Why not go get your reward and get a wagon and horse. We'll carry whatever we can and then be on our way."

"Sounds like a plan." Gisela said.

"I suppose so." Vincent added before he and Gisela went back to town.

Three days later the trio, along with Egis, were wheeling the wagon loaded with supplies and coin away from the cave. Gisela and Vincent rode their horses while Agota drove the wagon. Egis walked along the side of the wagon. Adventure called for the group and they all had hopes for the future. With a dragon pup they knew it would be difficult but Gisela didn't care about anything except finding glory. The giant's skull only did so much. Vincent wanted to find a purpose and Agota only wanted acceptance for Egis and for herself.

In time Gisela, Vincent, Agota and Egis would be known throughout the world and their friendship would forge a new world for many but that is another story for another time.

About the Author

Joseph S. Samaniego is a historian from North Carolina specializing in medieval European History. He has a Master of Arts in History and has future plans to receive a PhD.

In his daily life, he is not only a Fantasy author with 5 titles to his credit, he also writes non-fiction and is a gifted fantasy cartographer.

When he is not spending time with his family, Joseph spends time reading, writing and playing video games.